Divine Choreography of Redemption

Setting the Eternal Saga in Time

William E. Jefferson

HybridGlobal
PUBLISHING

Published by
Hybrid Global Publishing
301 E 57th Street, 4th fl
New York, NY 10022

Manufactured in the United States of America,
or in the United Kingdom when distributed elsewhere.

Jefferson, William E.
Divine Choreography of Redemption : Setting the Eternal Saga in Time
LCCN: 2018938707
ISBN: 978-1-948181-08-2
eBook: 978-1-948181-09-9

Cover design: Miriam Green
Cover photo: Steve Simmons
Interior design: Claudia Volkman

www.estillyen.com

Dedicated to Lois

CONTENTS

INTRODUCTION 1

PART ONE:
MIND'S EYE AND THE ALLURING LUMINOUS RINGS

ONE | Window in the Narrow Cove 7

TWO | Dreams and a Novel Idea 23

THREE | Mind's Eye and Weighing Words 31

PART TWO:
SURREAL LIFE OF THE OTHER ME

FOUR | All Saints and the Mysterious Visitors from Afar 41

FIVE | Seeing Redemption 53

SIX | Key Garden with Mr. Kind 71

SEVEN | Strange Brew—Bewilderment and the High Street Three 79

EIGHT | Stand at the Crossroads—"Look, Ask, Knock" 87

NINE | Keep Knocking—"I Know My Redeemer Lives" 99

TEN | Welcome to the Crimson Cliffs 109

ELEVEN | Divine Choreography of Redemption 121

TWELVE | The Manuscript 141

NOTES 149

INTRODUCTION

Beyond the Storied Sea, where mariners and pilgrims long to sail, lies the ancient Isle of Estillyen. Though equally far from everywhere, those who wish to explore the isle shall find it mystically near.

Still, a challenge awaits everyone who embarks on an Estillyen voyage. To reach the isle, one must willingly breach the Estillyen mist. Most pilgrims do so eagerly, but some voyagers choose to skirt the mist. Although close to their destination, they encounter the mist and simply refuse to enter. The mist confounds their wits, and they sail away.

Long ago, it's true, a strange incident occurred upon the isle. One clear Estillyen day, a thick veil of darkness rose out of the western sky, swept over the isle, and blotted out the sun. The darkness descended in a thick, hazy form that cloaked one and all. According to the reports, people moved about as "walking eyes," calling out to one another amidst the haze.

To counter the darkness, an iridescent mist spontaneously arose from the Storied Sea. At first the mist hovered faintly over the waves. Soon, however, broad swaths of shimmering mist encircled the isle a mile or so from shore. Then the mystical glow moved inland, consumed the darkness, and settled in, blanketing the isle with its reassuring presence.

Yet mystery remains. Many seafarers claim that in the dead of night, the Estillyen mist shimmers with a kind of frost-like light. In olden days sailors told of crewless crafts sailing amidst the mist. They swore that vessels suddenly appeared sporting long slender oars that sliced thorough the water in perfect harmony. Not a sailor or even a shadow on board—just oars sweeping past awestruck mariners taking in what they feared and saw.

Such sightings also tell of blissful figures dancing on the waves. Among them, a tale persists concerning a one-armed figure sporting a large

1

tambourine. As the story goes, the phantom bounced his tambourine fever-ishly from knee to knee until tears of joy filled his eyes. Then the rhythmic beats would cease and prolonged periods of silence would follow.

During such interludes, the percussionist would draw the tambourine tight to his chest and glide over the waters, as still as a statue soaking in the Estillyen mist. The most ardent believers of this long-held tale swear that the rolling sea flattened a path, aiding the phantom's passage.

No one knows, of course, what elements of truth rest in these ancient tales. Nevertheless folklore of this ilk nestles quite well in the nooks and crannies of everyday Estillyen life. It affords the isle a certain levity and mys-tery that pilgrims have long enjoyed.

Those who skirt the Estillyen mist miss the warm reception which awaits all who disembark in Port Estillyen. The skirters leave no footprints along Estillyen shores. Estillyen's noted monastery and abbey they do not tour. Nor do they watch sailboats chase about on Lakes Three.

At Gatherers Hall, where the skirters could have stayed, joyful pilgrims occupy their rooms, their beds. They sit at their tables in the dining hall. The pilgrims savor scrumptious fare the skirters might have shared.

Gatherers Hall strips away all comparisons in terms of culinary claim. Locals routinely observe departing guests sniffing the air, attempting to take in one last aromatic whiff emanating from the kitchen. Some visitors actu-ally weep upon departure, knowing they'll not savor delicacies so delightful again until they return to Estillyen.

Steeped in time, Estillyen possesses a very unique atmosphere, a distinct Estillyen-sphere. A rich communal spirit permeates the isle, pleasant to the core but subtly couched in the contemplative nature of Estillyenites. The complexion of the isle has a great deal to do with the Order of Message Mak-ers, founded in 1637 by a gentleman named Bevin Roberts.

Roberts' quiet impression and spiritual conviction afforded him a char-acter of noble humility. For twenty-nine years, Roberts and his troupe traveled throughout the continent giving dramatic readings drawn from Scripture nar-ratives. From tiny hamlets to vast hallowed halls, audiences eagerly gathered to take in Roberts' dramatic readings.

Then finally the day came when time laid its hands on Roberts and the troupe. No one knows the full press of circumstances, but outside a small village pub, Bevin Roberts suddenly stopped. As if commanded from on high, he halted. Roberts stood in the middle of the rutted street, raised his eyes of blue, and gazed down the long, jagged lane of darkened gray.

The late afternoon sun had slipped well behind the clouds and lay low in the winter sky.

A fierce, biting wind slapped Roberts in the face as the troupe huddled tight, their backs stiffened against the wind. They had spent a good portion of the afternoon on the inside of the pub, in front of an open fire, drawing warmth into their bones.

The troupe enjoyed a late, leisurely lunch and chatted freely. Yet they'd pause now and again to watch and listen to the embers crackle and hiss in the glowing hearth while ignoring the frosty windowpanes. The stilling moments fueled their musing minds.

The troupe knew their leader well, including how ardently Roberts had struggled with his voice's fade. The fading tone and lilt had become undeniable. During their most recent engagement, Roberts spoke his final lines almost inaudibly. Many in the audience leaned forward and cupped their ears in an attempt to hear what he had to say.

Roberts' condition had grown increasingly worse as winter set in, but among the troupe, the matter never surfaced in open discussion. On that cold afternoon Roberts surveyed his troupe, all bundled and ready. He doubted not their willingness, yet he knew full well their degree of weariness.

Eventually Roberts softly said, "Through the years we've traveled far, sowing seeds for gracious souls. In my mind's eyes, I behold the vast gallery of faces, ever present. Wonderful the sights we've seen, but none of them down to us. We must always remember the words of the psalmist, 'This is the Lord's doing; it is marvelous in our eyes.' His doing we have seen, not ours.

"Without a doubt time has brought us here today, but not to stay. I hear a bell in a distant tower. It beckons. Time has taken its toll. We must bid farewell to what we've known and enter what lies ahead.

"It's time to move on, time to welcome solitude and settle. Thus we shall strike out to find an isle of rest. For wise we must be in making moves that will forward the mission of our wordy mixes. Good-bye, yesterday! Yes, yes, good-bye. Let us greet tomorrow as if it had arrived today."

On February 4, 1637, as the record shows, Bevin Roberts and his troupe set foot on the Isle of Estillyen. There time moved at a slower pace. Months gave way to years, and years to decades. Eventually Bevin Roberts, like his voice, faded into time. One by one, the original troupe followed suit, yielding to the future present.

Yet their storytelling ways carried on, rooted deep in Estillyen soil. Today, the Message Makers of Estillyen dutifully carry on the work of Roberts and his troupe. The ancient texts of Scripture propel them. They have a way of becoming the message. As someone once said, "They have a knack for sticking words together in ways they don't normally run, to help you see things you don't normally see."

The message-making monks of Estillyen go by chosen names: Saga, Narrative, Plot, Story, and the like. Incidentally, I'm Story. Of course, all of our names relate to storytelling, which brings us quite naturally to our story, featuring my noted colleague Narrative.

PART ONE
Mind's Eye and the Alluring Luminous Rings

CHAPTER ONE
Window in the Narrow Cove

The day before yesterday, Brother Narrative conveyed to me in confidence a most interesting account. After hearing what he had to say, I asked Narrative to reconsider the matter of confidentially. Instinctively I felt the brothers should hear the story.

I also recommended that he put the account in writing. Narrative said he'd let me know the following day, which was yesterday. Today I received a note, along with a written document outlining his experience.

First the note:

Brother Story,
Much thanks for our time on Wednesday. Everyone needs a good listener.
I'm sure there's more to this saga than meets the eye. Just what, I'm not quite sure.
In keeping with your request, I submit, in writing, the essence of what I conveyed to you in person. Please feel free to share the following as you wish.
Peace,
Narrative

Next, Narrative's written account:

Quite late Tuesday night, I rose from my desk and peered out the leaded window in the narrow cove. As I neared the window, a cool stream of air seeped around the latched frame and fluttered past my cheek. Silently I stood gazing out from the cove.

The view of Port Estillyen never disappoints. The sight from my third-floor room always deposits something harmonious in my soul. I'm often drawn to the cove late, when the monastery sleeps. On Tuesday night I heard not a single creak, cough, or patter from the floors below.

I only heard the sound of wind softly whistling against the window, as if wishing to enter. My focus centered on the pools of light below the slender lampposts, lining the cobblestone street. My mind drifted from pool to pool, as it had so many times before.

Through the misty fog, the lampposts looked like stalwart sentinels. They appeared so upright, so dutiful, like guards riveted in place. A motionless scene I observed, except for a single soul who entered the first ring of light at the bottom of the lane. Aided by a cane, the lone figure walked with an elderly gait.

Slowly, on his way to somewhere, he passed through the luminous rings. Eventually he disappeared in darkness at the end of the lane. I wondered about his identity, his route, his reason for passing at this late hour. "Strange," I thought, "he looks like a discarnate soul, not an actual person." I wanted to see his face, say hello, but on he went to where he went.

While continuing to gaze upon the scene, I also noticed raindrops land on the diamond-shaped windowpanes. I studied how some drops would cling to the glass briefly, then let go and disappear along the leaded strips. Others moved in zigzag patterns, as if resisting the fall.

I thought, "Why do I think as I do?"[1] I reflected on our work and my good fortune of discovering the Order. Unwittingly, surprisingly, I had become a message maker, weaving words of stories old into works new. I thought, too, of Estillyen's inspirational setting, how it uniquely befits a storyteller.

Yet, I also felt perplexed, due to the fitful fray I had with words earlier in the day. Words of worth did not flow. Nor had they flowed for days that stretched back for weeks. Repeatedly I scrapped lines and phrases, along with scribbled pages. Through it all I began to question myself, my ability. I doubted not only my thoughts, but equally my doubts.

As I stood before the window, a line from King Lear came to mind: "Who is that can tell me who I am?"[2] A faint smile crept upon my face.

Why I smiled, I don't know. I confess, a tinge of lunacy touched me. I saw my face reflected in two of the innermost windowpanes. A strip of lead ran diagonally across my right cheek. The strip sliced my portrait in half.

With my smile cut in two, I smiled the more and managed a soft chuckle. Consequently, I bent my knees and framed my face in a lower pane. The lead strip had gone, but the wavy glass transposed my chin into an elongated V. So I rose and centered my face in an upper pane. No longer distorted or slit in two, my face appeared perfectly framed. However, another strip of lead severed my head.

I decided to disregard my fractured image in the panes and once again focused on the lights along the lane. The pools of light on the vacant cobblestone street provided a perfect backdrop for a mind in need of repose. Then into the quiet moment, the foyer hall clock sent forth strikes that echoed up the stairs. Strike followed strike until the twelfth had struck. I knew Wednesday had arrived.

Not wanting to move amidst the chimes, I waited for silence. When it arrived, I stepped from the window and returned to my desk. Despite the hour, a steady stream of thoughts continued to race through my mind. I determined to wrestle on, to pen them down.

I scribbled away, filling and bending pages over the top of the pad. After a while I quit and pondered what I had scrolled. Somehow I felt assured that the lines would read better in the light of day, swiftly approaching. At that point, the tall clock dispensed its double strike. So I rose, clicked off the light, and navigated to bed.

Comforted by the weight of the covers, I closed my eyes, slowly exhaled, and fell fast asleep. Then, near half past three, I awoke to a stream of light dancing on the ceiling. The light stretched across the ceiling and part way down the wall. The streaming light emanated from the window in the cove and widened in proportion to its distance from the window.

The spectacle I had witnessed before. Yet this time tree limb shadows dueled away in the stream of light, creating a mesmerizing effect in the darkened room. After a moment or so, I peeled back the covers and slipped out of bed. As I stepped toward the window, the stream of light on the ceiling steadily retreated with me. Ultimately the light illuminated just the window and my frame.

Staring on, out of the corner of my eye I saw something move. To my surprise, the lone figure that had appeared earlier reappeared. Just as before, one by one, he passed through the rings of light. Although instead of disappearing into the darkness at the end of the lane, he stepped into the final ring.

There, in the center of the ring, he turned around and looked up at the monastery, directly toward my window, or so it seemed to me. Next he raised his cane in a sweeping motion, as if signaling someone to follow. No one came forth because no one followed. Again he signaled with his cane, but this time with a motion more hurriedly.

I thought, "Surely his gestures have nothing to do with me." To assure myself, I whispered, "Surely not," only to respond by asking myself, "Why not?" Clearly he continued to stare in my direction. For a third time he offered his sweeping motion. I could almost hear him say, "Come on, come on."

I shut my eyes, thinking I had dreamed the sight. Then the inexplicable occurred. When I opened my eyes, I saw myself hurriedly exiting the monastery's front entrance. Believe me, even if you don't. I'm telling the truth.

While still in the cove, I watched myself move into another sphere. I had become both witness and participant. In the first person, I acted; in the third person, I observed.

Insane, I know. Nevertheless I swear that I watched myself race from the entrance. I had a curious look on my face, rather resolute. I swiftly moved along the path, but by the time I reached the pools of light, the stranger had gone.

I called, but no one answered. Consequently I passed through the final ring of light, thinking I'd still find him. At the end of the lane, I entered the darkness, only to find it lit. I had stepped into a sphere beyond, a world I knew well, yet not at all.

All that I experienced would take too long to tell. So, succinctly I'll summarize. When I entered Port Estillyen's high street, the thoroughfare swelled with visitors mingling among the locals. At the west end of the street, a vendor from Fields and Crops sold chips, but no fish; no one asked for fish. Chips alone seemed perfectly normal. I felt an insatiable appetite for fish.

I moved on to McGowan's Flower Shop and Bakery. I'd never seen the shops so packed. Strangely, my senses operated both inside the premises as well as out. As I watched customers sniffing roses at the flower shop, somehow I could smell what the sniffers smelled. At the bakery, when a shopper picked up a loaf of bread, my fingers felt the crust. It seemed totally unreal, but not at all frightening.

I continued on, making my way through the high street hubbub. Each scene appeared as real as day, except for the time of day. Oddly, I couldn't distinguish day from night. The entire panorama appeared backlit.

Further, no one seemed to notice me, or me noticing them. Like at a carnival or fair, people stood along the high street listening to vendors calling out to the crowds. People eagerly moved along, swapping places.

At the three main attractions, people pressed in close to hear and watch the staged presenters. These attractions drew hundreds of spectators. Although the exhibits ran right next to each other, the sound from one did intrude on the other. Again I thought, "How odd."

At the edge of each crowd, people gathered in little huddles, chatting incessantly. The intensity of speech struck me, as if everyone spoke at once, without listening. I tried to grasp words and lines, but conversing lips moved too swiftly. I caught a few phrases now and then, but not the meaning conveyed. Communication didn't really matter. Chatter for chatter's sake served both the means and the end.

Before long, I left the chattering behind and worked my way into the first of the main attractions. I maneuvered into the crowd, but soon pressing bodies locked me in near the middle of the mass.

Next to me, a mother stood with her teenage daughter. We faced the front, with a good view of the raised stage. A bold red banner with white lettering stretched tightly across the rostrum. The banner read "Platform Building."

Within a couple of minutes, a bald-headed man stepped forward, wearing high-riding gold trousers, a white shirt, and a dark green vest. The man's presence instantly galvanized the crowd. I looked around to see bulging eyes and attentive faces, as a hush settled in.

The speaker approached an old-fashioned metal mic, clutched the stand,

and began to speak. "Hello, folks," he said. "Good to see you here, at this particular place. You've arrived perfectly on time. No moment, of any hour, could be better than the moment now. Fate has found you, brought you.

"So don't be shy; press in close and even closer still. I'm not here to obfuscate the truth. I've come to illuminate the wonders of technopoly, how technique can think for us.[3] Come near, all who feel disenfranchised and benched by life. You must get back in the game, and get in to win, which you shall.

"I speak to you today of good fortune—your good fortune. Yes indeed, benefactors of fortune; that's who I see standing before me. What's that you say? Continue, continue—I shall, don't worry. Your presence emboldens me and reassures my conviction.

"My mission is a matter of upmost importance. I offer not a hocus-pocus elixir, but words. Yes, certainly, substantive words that will undergird and lift you. I offer you my word, in words. What more can I say? Two words, I suppose, the words I now propose. Two of the most important words you'll ever here: *Platform Building.*

"Please, listen up; reject not the waves that resonate in your zone of hearing. I'm speaking to you about *Platform Building in the Age of Technopoly.* Yes, that's it, the very title of my most recent book. Technopoly, you ask, what's that? 'Technopoly is a state of culture. It is also a state of mind.'[4] The focus is grand, not granular.

"In our modern age of technopoly, the grand instruments of technology aid us in aiding them. With technology we coexist, coevolve, and codevelop the world of tomorrow, which is here today. We now live in the era of digital narratives, which are creative amalgams of 'human intuition and emotion with machine logic.'[5]

"Technology helps us authenticate and authorize our cultural quests. Technology brings out our true potential, lifting us from peasants to potentates of human trajectory. As a late scholar once said, 'We find our satisfaction in technology, and take orders from technology.'[6]

"So right, so very right it is. Which would you prefer, an ill-tempered, shortsighted, know-it-all boss with ulcers telling you what to do, or a reasoned glass cube that offers options? Forget the days of roulette wheels. They are as outmoded as cornerstones and rock foundations. Forget, too, those who run around saying we live in an age of information glut. Do you feel gluttonous by what you know?

"Take it from me; we are destined to proceed in the manner we have been progressing. We must proceed 'under the assumption that information is our friend, believing that cultures may suffer grievously from lack of information, which of course, they do.'[7] Build your unique platform on cubes of glass that process information as fast as light chasing light. Face the facts, 'The deck is stacked, economically and emotionally, in automation's favor.'[8]

"Don't worry about all the vicissitudes that arise in the age of technopoly. A model for the new world is now emerging. Our species is trending toward Neom, a future new.[9] Not a future chained to the pessimistic past, but a breakaway future led by technological advancement. 'Neom is a place for dreamers who want to create something new in the world, something extraordinary.'

"With the right platforms to aid you, make you, you can crest the waves of the future new with great agility. You must, however, learn the proper techniques of platform building. You must be known, not unknown. You must steer clear of sentimental bogs and mossy, retreaded legends.

"Listen, please, I know full well what it means to be tired of being you. I, too, was like you, tired of being me, in a manner handed down by history. Weighed down by life's gravitational force, I trudged along in boggy valleys of death, where the sun sets but never rises. Unseen, unknown, alone, you trudge through the boggy valley facing death, but for what?

"The time has come for you to climb up out of that boggy, shadowy valley. *Platform Building in the Age of Technopoly* will teach you the art of making yourself known. Discover the true art of building an image of yourself, which is not yourself—and needn't be.

"Everything is different now. Being known for what you do is far more important than what you do. In fact, that's the most important thing to do. Become known; free yourself from anonymity and the servitude bogs laid down by man. Blog!

"Consider your image; care for it. It depends on you to promote it. In turn, your image can do more for you than you can ever do for you. Ask not what you can do for your image. That's the old-school way, the way without reward. Instead ask what your image can do for you. It's so right that it nudges toward righteousness. My words underlie the truth of reciprocity.

"Let us be clear. I know each of you shares the grief and sorrow of the poor and needy among us. We must grieve with the grievers, mourn with the mournful. It is meet and right so to do, and a joyful endeavor too. However, hear this, and hear it sure: the very best you can do for the least of these is to model what they, too, can be. Model their dreams. Build your platform for the world to see.

"Hear me, my friends; this is the age of technoploy, of social connections without needless communicative interjections, of companionship without the demands of communion.[10] Intense dialogue has it place, but in many quarters it's now passé. From your platform in the social sphere, your image can soar with lighthearted flight. Boundless are the spheres awaiting you.

"Know this: I'm with you in this redemptive quest. I live for you, whether you're for me or against me. My aim is to complete my course and run the race destiny has prescribed. In sharing the efficacy of platform building, each day I rise and my pace quickens. Weariness shall never catch me.

"I've expended my all, so to speak, in setting forth the wonders of *Platform Building in the Age of Technopoly*. Yet I've done so delightfully, despite much hardship and pushback from taskmasters of rotting narratives. To know that I've contributed to the betterment of mankind shall be my reward, my only reward. You are my reward, if you are willing to be rewarded.

"Yes, you've heard correctly. So hear! 'The world of the ear is more embracing and inclusive than that of the eye can ever be.'[11] Despise not sage advice that resonates in your eardrums and seeks to settle in your soul. Depart, I tell you, from your selfish, myopic, private, self-serving ways. Instead devote yourself to your platform. Serve it with an un-timorous heart.

"The central tenant of my philosophy is clear. Lay down your burden of self, and fix your eyes on your platform. Serve it, nurture it, and let your image go where you shall never go. And get this: your image will have followers, scads of followers following, and followers following them. It doesn't matter where your image goes; the point is being there.

"My book will teach you how to harness the perfect apps for building your unique platform. You owe it to your image; don't enslave your hopeful projection. If you are for your image, and your image is for you, who can be against you? Even the undertaker can't take you under. Your image will be bequeathed to you in a manner of reciprocity.

"My friends, today if you have ears to hear, despise not your rendezvous with destiny. Wait no longer; time is ticking; today is the day of platform building, now is the accepted time. What you are waiting for is waiting for you. Pick up a copy of *Platform Building in the Age of Technopoly* and follow me. Surrender yourself; build your platform.

"You haven't a moment to lose. This morning, in anticipation of your eagerness, I received a ready supply of my new book. How many do I have? I'm not sure, but enough. We'll crack open the crates and let you have at 'em. You shall not go away empty-handed, and you'll not be refused. Now, just step over to the right of the stage where my assistants . . ."

As the green-vested man carried on, I freed myself from the crowd. Stunned, and jarred emotionally, I tried to make sense of what I'd just experienced. As I broke free from the audience, I paused and closed my eyes. I thought the insanity might wash away. I breathed slowly; it felt good to breathe. I had to breathe.

When I opened my eyes, what I saw took my breath away. Shocked, I found myself in the middle of the adjacent crowd. Everyone jockeyed for position, trying to get near the stage. En masse, the crowd pressed forward.

A tall, skinny man sporting a wireless head mic suddenly appeared. With velvety ease, he moved to the center of the platform and positioned himself in front of a large assortment of blank screens. Arrayed on boxes and stands, the screens covered the entire width of the platform.

For nearly a minute, the man spoke not a word. He simply stood in place, smiling pleasantly and gazing down at crowd. As the seconds ticked away, the audience jittered with anticipation. Then the thin man glanced at his watch, stretched out his arms, and brought his bony hands together with a sharp clap. Instantly, all the screens lit up, each displaying the topic of his message: Discarnate Life.

At that, he began to speak. "Yes, discarnate life—that's precisely the topic I'm compelled to present to you today. You, me, all of us have already

grown 'accustomed to substituting an abstract image for [our] physical being. In fact, twentieth-century man—electronic man—has lived minus a physical body for an entire century.'[12]

"Now we must progress, move on into the wondrous world of discarnate
life awaiting us. Dampen neither your enthusiasm nor your expectations.
Let them soar, and rightly so. You stand not at a precipice awaiting your fall.
You face a most propitious way of life: discarnate life.

"As I've traveled throughout this fair city port, I can see that in every
way you are a most ambitious people. You are the sort of people who strive,
who thrive on striving. I trust that my message on discarnate life will find
welcome receptivity. I'm sure it will. This new vista of augmented, discarnate life is as important as life itself. The future has arrived to gift us, to
carry us where we were destined to be.

"Know this: my words rise from a well of deep conviction. I speak of
our spiritual sensibilities, how your spirit innately longs to break free of its
carnate cage. There can be no greater human virtue than that quest. What
are virtues of love, joy, and peace without quest? Quest is twined with reach.
Reach out your hands, look at them; you are more than physical."

At that juncture he paused and looked at his hands, as someone
might do in examining a rash. Amazingly almost everyone in crowd followed suit. They looked at their hands, stupefied, as if reading the pattern
of their palms.

"What I say to you is this. You must transcend the here-and-now now,
not wait for legendary chariots and trumpet blasts. Reach, and accept no
shame in your quest for discarnate life. Discarnate life is one of the chief
wonders of life. The old has gone, the new has arrived, and without quest
you have nothing. Fallacious notions of limited human capacity have no
domain in discarnate life. Shake free of your fuzzy faculties.

"Century after century our ancestors accepted their laborious lot of toil-
ing and tilling in the soil, with little hope of breaking free of the spade. No
longer! A new providential hand has been dealt to this generation. I shall
not beat about the pauper's patch.

"It comes down to this, pure and simple. By embracing stale narratives
of the past, you have demented your ascendance. Forget it. Move on, reach,

and embrace the quest. Embrace discarnate life. Today a new defining narrative begins—live it; go discarnate.

"Yes, that's correct—discarnate. In doing so, your vistas will extend beyond your wildest dreams. You don't belong to the school of loony Luddites, the 'machine breakers' who wrongfully believed that automation impaired the human race.[13] You belong to the wondrous age of algorithms. The wisest move we can make is to 'defer to the wisdom of algorithms.'[14]

"Oh, the very sound of the word thrills me. It dissects so nicely: *al-go-rithms*. Repeat after me that charming noun aiding discarnate life—*algorithms*."

To my amazement, everyone in the crowd simultaneously belted, "*Algorithms*."

"Again," he said, and again the crowd replied, "*Algorithms*."

The fervent reply unnerved me. I wanted to evade the thin man's line of sight, so I hid my face behind the gentleman's head in front of me. I peeked around his right ear, exposing only my right eye to the stage.

Once again the thin man riveted the crowd's attention with a single, sharp clap. Instantly his image filled the screens. His every move the screens projected. The crowd looked on, enthralled.

He went on, "Today, I challenge you to free yourself from your carnate cage, your carnate state," he said. "You belong to the age of algorithms. Oh, just the sound of the word. Repeat after me, *algorithms*.

"You've not waltzed into this gathering unobserved. You have been called, chosen. Automation and reality are in full embrace, like reach and quest. They are inseparable. Advancements in technology have increased our human worth. Oh, what a wondrous time to be alive, no longer bound to a carnate cage!

"Daily the rush of mediated messages propels us. Beneath the invisible cloud we move and transcend our being. We eagerly cast off everything that hinders our mediated quest, lying hold of our apps and indispensable devices.[15] Swiftly we race away from the old mammoth age of centuries past, which lacked the modern accoutrements and the promise of discarnate life.

"Reach, grasp this truth, and grasp it well. We live in the era of wide-eyed expectation. The center ring of human history is ours; it belongs to no one else. Our space in time upon this planet has no comparison. All of history has longed and waited to behold the *here* and *now* we possess, our age of mediated advancement, algorithms, and discarnate life.

"Media extend the face of man, the voice of man, and, might I say, the meaning of man. They showcase to all the principalities and powers of time and space our true carnate and discarnate potential—combined in a way the world has never witnessed. 'The simultaneity of electric communication, also characteristic of our nervous system, makes each of us present and accessible to every other person in the world.'[16] Isn't that wonderous?

"The Urim and the Thummim have no place in our age of algorithms. Think about it. What other generations longed for, you have. Together we stand upon the summit of history, not in the lost ruins of yesteryear. We are not to be defined by the base term *Homo erectus*. If you believe you are dust, awaiting dust's return, naturally you will be predisposed to earthy forces.

"But I say to you, there's far more to you than ribs and sinews. You have yet to grasp your true potential. Let your aspirations extend to the heavens. Slip on the goggles of vistas new. Strap round your wrists your most treasured devices. Connect and take in the wonders of discarnate life.

"Lay hold of devices new. Never tire of doing so; they will never tire of you. 'Technologhy enchants' so be enchanted.[17] Rush out to embrace them as soon as they arrive. They will comfort you, companion you, and not abandon you. When you lie down at night, your devices will rest near, recharge, and await your rise.

"When you awake, they awaken with you. They help you stream into the stratosphere. No longer are you bound by boundaries of stale narratives. Unfettered, your face will float in space. Your voice will echo among the stars. Your words will stream on and on as a testament to your liberated state. Don't worry; your carnate being 'is still there, tucked away somewhere, in one the locations, but it is irrelevant to the new condition of multi-locationalism.'[18]

"Don't look back. Look ahead. And don't let your hearts be troubled; the entire cosmos is your community. Algorithms will never leave or forsake you. Under the cloud, you will never want for direction. Whether you turn to the right or the left, algorithms will speak to you, enlighten your path, telling you the way you should go.

"What's also true is this: you don't give up your ability to choose. Algorithms simply help you choose your choices. Hear me, friends, I implore you. Move out of your old, tired, carnal state into your new discarnate existence."

With that statement lobbed, I felt faint, sick. I spun free of the audience. I needed air. Just beyond the crowd, I found a wooden telephone pole. I placed my back against the splintered object and tilted my face to the sky. The pole felt reassuring, solid. I welcomed the splinters pressing against my shoulders and ribs.

I could have stayed there indefinitely, but I didn't linger long. A buzz of excitement emanated from crowd three. I felt drawn, though drunk mentally and confused. Somehow I maneuvered my way into the gathering.

I pretended to belong. Standing in the center of the crowd, I looked to my left and right, only to see everyone staring straight ahead. In no time, a white-haired gentleman walked onstage, bearing a wry smile.

The man appeared more thick than thin, slightly stout. Nevertheless the crowd beheld an imposing figure, a stern-looking man, sort of like a sergeant. His demeanor offered no comedic gestures.

The stout man stepped across the stage and halted beneath three lights spaced about a meter apart. Long black cords extended the lights from a boxed beam above. The lights had red metal shades that swayed in the breeze. Consequently the light rhythmically danced back and forth across the white-haired figure.

The man's eyes were set deep in his face, sheltering them from the light. Their color I could not detect. Behind him, a banner the width of the stage boasted a single word: redemption. In crimson red, the noun appeared, on a white background that made it stark. Posturing himself, like a captain on deck, the man cleared his throat and began to speak.

"Welcome, ladies and gentlemen, and anyone else who does not fit that description. I welcome you, one and all. A single word defines the subject of my address: *redemption*.

"No doubt curiosity has drawn you here. And might I say, curiosity never killed the cat; the cat died for lack of curiosity. Eventually too weak to move, the cat starved to death. Such weakness in you I do not see.

"Many have longed to see what you long to see, to hear what you have longed to hear. Billions have come and gone, without attaining proper revelation. It saddens my soul, grievously so, to see the masses suffer.

"We all need redemption, do we not? Seeking redemption is a noble aim. In time, want and sorrow make their rounds to each of us. So I say to you, do not despise the gurney that carries you from the field of battle. It can save your life, and possibly your soul.

"This day I lay before you life and death, hope and despair. Pair them as you wish; they are yours to choose. Yes, certainly you need redemption; we all need redemption.

"However, the redemption I propose is not the kind you suppose.

"The redemption I set before you is not the old-fashioned kind, parceled out by sacrificing bullocks, rams, and turtledoves. Nor is it the new old-fashioned kind, formed on that rocky outcrop called Golgotha. Those ancient narratives are for yesteryear, for time spent.

"Don't get me wrong, the old tales have their place for certain in museums and such. Who doesn't like to glance at an intriguing artifact now and then? I do, though fleetingly. But I ask you, what do the bones from some old ditch in Jerusalem or Jericho have to do with you? Likewise, how can an old papyrus fragment assist your earthly sojourn?

"The answer is, not a lot. The days of hand-me-down faith and old-school religion are swiftly passing. Practicing religion, rooted in bygone days, amounts to constriction of human liberty. Why should your offspring gnaw on old relics, when a smorgasbord of knowledge awaits their discovery?

"These, my friends, are the days of buoyancy, not drudgery, days of picking and choosing your preferred path via the broad path paved by information. And the path of which I speak is clearly a better way. It leads to a freer future. I speak of facts, not fantasy.

"The central point, which I'm passing on to you, is simply this—the redemption you truly need is to be redeemed from the notion of redemption. That truth, in and of itself, is true redemption.

"Oh, the vista of liberation that awaits you! Consider it: free to think, reason, and reject anything that stands in the way of your future present. Yes, I spoke correctly: your future is present, if you have the will to embrace it.

"Friends and foe alike, I call upon you to depart from your bowing and genuflecting ways. Stand tall; breath deep. I'm here to warn you, not to harm you. Vicious wolves seek out timid sheep, particularly those known for pious, genuflecting rituals. Their antics give them away, and they end up in the wolf's lair.

"Therefore, make up your mind, and let your mind make you. All you will ever need you already have, if only you have the reason and good sense to possess it. Think, and know, this hour may never come your way again. Shake off the archaic shackles that have bound you. Wriggle free from your chains of delusion, and be redeemed by the renewing of your mind.

"Yes, your mind and you, you and your mind—don't you see, I propose a path of common sense. Whatever you do, do not ignore your common sense aligned with your physical being. Stick with your brains. If you allow yourself to listen to that idea of soul searching, you have fallen into the lap of the poets.

"Then what? Poets are tricky; their words always have two meanings, often more. Everyone reading poetry experiences a 'poem differently as his or her sensibility conforms to the poetic situation provided by the poet.'[19] In so doing, you have entered the land of fairies, not facts. Let your mind make you, and information make your mind.

"I say again, the only redemption you truly need is to be redeemed from the notion of redemption.

"This very hour . . ."

How long he went on, I do not know. I desperately wanted to escape, somehow, somewhere. I ran down the high street, turned down Bridgeport Lane, and did not look back. On I hurried, seeking a way out of the mysterious affair.

Eventually, I watched myself disappear in the fog at the end of Market Street. Then I snapped to. I recall nothing more.

Yet a stream of clarity flowed through my mind . . .

CHAPTER TWO
Dreams and a Novel Idea

Brother Story continues . . .

Sometime before daybreak Narrative had dropped by Scribe House and slipped his letter through the office door mail chute. When I entered the office this morning, I immediately spotted the envelope in the wire cage affixed to the door. The letter stood upright in the otherwise empty cage.

The chunkiness of the envelope surprised me. I expected merely a page or two from Narrative, recounting his experience. At any rate, I retrieved the letter, and, in the early morning quiet, I began to read about the incident that had captured his mind.

I proceeded slowly, pausing routinely. I found the content gripping, yet challenging to process. Not because I disbelieved the account. I believed it fully, but I wanted to understand what had actually taken place.

This I knew, and only this: something most peculiar had happened to Brother Narrative.

Initially my suspicion centered on a dream. The whole affair sounded completely otherworldly. If not a dream, then what? Yes, what? Could the answer point to psychosis? I wondered if Narrative had suffered a breakdown of some sort. Yet nothing in his demeanor warranted this conclusion.

Nevertheless, I made copies of Narrative's letter and circulated them to the brothers: Epic, Saga, Plot, Writer, and Drama. I knew the situation would both puzzle and concern them. Especially Narrative's last line: "Yet a stream of clarity flowed through my mind . . ." What clarity could emerge from such a bizarre experience?

In our monastic community, it doesn't take long for the brothers to gather, when they have a mind to do so. Within an hour of receiving the letter, Writer had arrived and occupied the lone empty chair across from my desk. A few minutes later Drama and Plot joined us. Shortly thereafter Saga arrived, with Epic on his heels.

Everyone clutched a copy of Narrative's epistle. We shifted around and decided to huddle around the refectory table in the adjoining room. Once seated, we began to exchange pleasantries. "Coffee, no tea, thanks." Smiling and stirring spoons, we gestured on, as if prepping ourselves for the topic at hand. Drama looked toward me, as did Saga, but I didn't want to start the discussion. Eventually Plot spoke up. "Story, we're all here with Narrative's letter, minus the letter writer. Is he planning to join us? I haven't seen him since early prayers."

"No, I didn't invite him," I replied. "Actually, I didn't invite anyone because I didn't know we were meeting."

"That's right," Drama said.

"Did Narrative know his document would be decimated?" Epic asked.

"Yes, sure," I said. "We talked about it yesterday. He seemed keen to discuss the episode. He's rather engrossed in the whole affair."

"I've never read anything quite like it," Writer said; "it's truly extraordinary. Do you believe it's all in his head, a kind of augmented collaboration of learning and vision? Antagonists quoting works . . . it's a bit stupefying."

"I know," I said. "But this is not something Narrative has conjured up. Or perhaps I should say, if he has conjured it up, he certainly doesn't know he has."

"The man with a cane," Saga said. "It reminds me of the character described by Goodwin and Hollie Macbreeze. You know, that elderly gentleman they met in Century as they waited for the Estillyen ferry."

"Could be, who knows," Drama said.

"This seems strange coming from Narrative," I said. "Among us, he's considered the most down to earth—you know what I mean. He's likely the brightest as well.

"Those antagonists he described," Drama said. "What utterly amazing, scary figures; they possessed such rivaling ideas."

"*Possessed* is the right word," Writer said.

"We need to talk with him," Plot said. "See if he's all right. Likely he's at the shore wondering about us, what we think of his letter."

"You are probably right, Plot," I said.

Few locations on the isle offer more serenity than the stretch of Misty Shore, extending along the base of the Point. It's said that the spot has a way of recalibrating the soul. Saga and Epic couldn't break away, so Writer, Drama, Plot, and I decided make the trek. We agreed to meet up at the fork to Misty Shore in an hour. As it turned out, each of us arrived early.

We spotted Narrative at a distance. He sat on a large boulder, calmly staring down at the splashing waves and holding a book in his hand. He glanced in our direction, spotted us, and resumed his pose. When we drew near, I said, "We're looking for three suspicious characters described in a letter. Any chance you've seen 'em?"

Narrative straightened up, smiled, and said, "Greetings! You must be worried about me. Have a seat; share the boulder."

"Well, if it's possible to worry without being worried," I said, "that would describe us, I suppose. We just wanted to see you . . . and chat."

"Beautiful spot this time of day," Writer said. "Or for that matter, any time of day."

"Yes, I love it," Narrative said.

"What are you reading?" Plot asked.

"Ellul—an old work. I pull it out now and again to see what I've underlined and circled.

"I love this bit: 'Day after day the wind blows away pages of our calendars, our newspapers, and our political regimes, and we glide along the stream of time without any spiritual framework, without a memory, without a judgment, carried about by "all winds of doctrine" on the current of history, which is always slipping into a perpetual past.'"[20]

"I'd say that sort of syncs with your letter," Drama said.

"I suppose it does," Narrative said. "I didn't compose it, though. I mean, I wrote the letter, but I didn't sit down and dream up the scenes. I saw them; I walked among them . . . such an experience. Do you think I've gone mad?"

"Well, let's skip that part," Drama said. "We're all mad, in one way or another."

"Everyone's received your letter, Nar," I said. "We discussed it a bit at the office. Epic and Saga wanted to come along, as well, but we told them we'd catch them on the return. Saga needed to check in on Dr. Paterson. Ninety-eight and still with us, but it looks like he'll be departing soon."

"I know," Narrative said. "I passed by his room yesterday. I didn't enter; he was fast asleep."

"Your experience, Nar," Writer said. "We're kind of gobsmacked. What do you make of it?"

"Not exactly sure," Narrative said. "I believe it happened, but *what* happened—that's the tricky part."

"So you're serious, taking this to heart?" Plot asked.

"Yes, whatever that means," Narrative said. "You know me; I'm not the jokey type. I'd never go on like this on a whim."

"I see," Drama said. "Well, I'm sure it won't be as hard to decipher as the thunder in *Finnegans Wake*."

We continued to lob questions at Narrative, but our efforts produced only stutters and stops. Narrative, we could tell, wanted a more thoughtful discussion. I suggested we head back to Gatherers' Hall for a cup of tea. Narrative gladly agreed. Plot sped along to catch up with Epic and Saga.

Some forty minutes later, all seven of us occupied a round table for eight at the hall. With steaming cups of tea set out before us, the conversation commenced anew.

"So you've all read it?" Narrative asked.

"Yes," Drama said, as the rest of us nodded and blinked our eyes in reply.

"I do feel all jumbled, you know," Narrative said. "Really, it's so unreal . . . but real . . ."

"What would you like to hear from us?" I asked.

"Don't know, for sure," he replied. "Just talk, I suppose."

"Well, what about the stream of clarity?" I asked.

"Yes, that's important," Narrative said. "But let me hold that for a minute, if you don't mind."

"As you like," Epic said.

We topped up our cups and sipped away, as Narrative continued. He eventually came around to the point undergirding his true concern.

"My work on redemption," he said. "Somehow lately I've felt constrained about the whole idea of a book. When I pick up my pen, it feels like it belongs to someone else. I honestly question if it's right for me to do what I've set out to do."

"What are you saying?" Drama asked. "Do you want to scrap the project after all the time and energy you've invested?"

"No . . . well, maybe. It's not the theme that worries me. We all agree: the focus on redemption as divine drama is timely. We need to do more with it in our readings, maybe partner with St. Agnes. What does Balthasar say? 'Our play "plays" in his play.'[21] I think that's it.

"Anyway, as I said, it's not the theme; it's *me* that worries me. In particular, the pronoun *I*, as in *me*—that worries me."

"I see," Drama said.

"Narrative," I said, "help us understand where you're going with this. And your unusual dream, or experience—how does that fit?"

He said, "Dream, vision, or whatever I saw—I saw something I needed to see. I experienced something in another sphere, life on another plane.

"On the first stage, I saw a vain figure. 'Discover the true art of building an image of yourself, which is not yourself, and needn't be.' He spoke those lines with such delight.

"Not a word about ultimate purpose or meaning. 'Devote yourself to your platform. Serve it with an un-timorous heart.' All too true, this construct. His words made me shudder.

"Next, the thin man surrounded by screens took the stage. He extolled the wonders of discarnate life. With riveted eyes, the crowd watched his every move. If he'd told them to leap into his screens, I'm sure they would have tried.

"I felt sick as he spoke. 'I challenge you to free yourself from your carnate cage, your carnate state,' he said. 'You belong to the age of algorithms. Oh, the very sound of the word thrills me. It dissects so nicely: *al-go-rithms*. Repeat after me that charming noun aiding discarnate life—*algorithms*.'

"His words echoed through an audience of open ears. The interest of the crowd grew with his every word. They looked like spectators waiting for a rocket launch.

"The third speaker offered the most treacherous message of all. The white-haired man stood beneath the swaying lights, commanding the stage. He looked like a stand-in for Beelzebub himself. Proudly he set out his premise. 'The only redemption you truly need is to be redeemed from the notion of redemption.'

"To my utter amazement, smiles swept across the crowd of faces. The glib joy with which he spoke shocked me. 'Rocky outcrop called Golgotha,' he said with a smirk on his face.

The entire scene was swarming with dissonance."

"OK, Narrative, but what about the clarity?" I asked.

"Well, I feel clear about my impressions, if that helps," he said. "First, I don't want to build my platform. The book, the theological work . . . the task is not mine alone. It belongs to all of us.

"The second thought centers on the power of mediated messages. They swirl round about us at an unrelenting pace. They mold and make us, alarm and harm us. It's true: we serve the tools we make.[22] We can't go back in time. We don't want to go back. The question is: where are we going?

"Again, the speaker with his discarnate message touched on reality. The reality, however, centers on the reality of discarnate souls. They're on the rise, if you will pardon the pun.

"My third impression centers on redemption. There is no subject more important. What we know we need to make known. As message makers, we need to help people practice the art of peering *through* the lines of Scripture, to see their part in the divine drama.

"If, indeed, 'all the world's a stage,'[23] it's comforting to know there's a divine eye that sees the drama through."

"OK, Narrative," I said. "We've listened attentively. What do you recommend?"

"Not sure," he said. "I still see a book, just not the one I envisioned. With your consent, I'd like to switch genres, try a fictional approach, but one full of meaning. Also, as I said, the work needs to be from all of us, the Estillyen Message Makers. Not just me. I want to be absolved from the pronoun *I*, as in *me* or *my*.

"I'm willing to draft the manuscript. Then you can rip it apart and help piece it together."

"OK, interesting," I said. "How does everyone feel? Any objections?"

"Not a problem with me," Epic said.

"Me neither," Drama said.

Plot said, "I'm all for it."

Writer and Saga said nothing, but looked pleased with the idea.

"If you have a mind to do it, we're confident you're the one to do it," I said. "How long do you suppose it will take?"

"Don't know; who can say?" Narrative said.

From there we carried on, until the twin earthen-brown teapots had nothing more to pour and our cups of tea had been sipped away.

A sense of affirmation emerged from the discussion, along with an air of excitement about Narrative's proposal. We know him; we love him. We felt certain he would offer something quite interesting to read.

Narrative wasted little time in getting on with his novel idea. We saw him daily, of course, at prayers, during chores and meals. However, as time went on, we watched him pass into deepening degrees of otherworld absorption.

The same cheerful Narrative greeted us each day with a ready smile, but his eyes betrayed the intensity working in his mind. While looking straight at us, we could see him looking beyond us. With the mind's eye, he saw a world unseen.

Narrative lived in two worlds, ours and another far removed. We knew, in time, we would discover his true whereabouts in our world and out.

Though I'm Story, the rest of story belongs to Narrative. It's his to tell.

CHAPTER THREE
Mind's Eye and Weighing Words

Narrative's Account

Shortly after the roundtable tea with the brothers, I seriously began to question the novel approach. The content, the setting . . . how would this novel materialize? I had neither an outline, nor a single page drafted. What did I expect—chapters sprouting like wild mushrooms?

No doubt my otherworld experience had profoundly affected me. It catapulted me into a new way of thinking about what could be seen and said. I felt freed from the erudite shackles and techniques offering limited appeal. I wanted to reach the high street filled with public faces. I wanted to see watching eyes and ears listening.

I merely needed to grasp the nettle and find my voice in this new panorama of novel creativity. So the nettle I grasped, but a novel about redemption refused to form pages upon my desk. As days passed, I repeatedly caught myself staring into the mirror. I'd peer into my eyes, hoping to see the spark of creativity. I saw only peering eyes.

I questioned myself repeatedly about choosing a fictional approach. I felt uncomfortably numb, flippant. At times I'd drill myself particularly hard. Especially when standing in front of the medicine cabinet mirror. The medicine cabinet, for me, represented a kind of gut reality. It made me feel basic, common, and honest about my senses.

I had never written a novel, and now a blank novel awaited my achievement. I'd pen a line or two, and then another. It was along the lines of, "Begin where you wish in considering the drama of redemption, and forfeit not your part upon the stage. Know that each and every soul plays the part they play."

I would moan and scrap the lines. I couldn't start, not really in a manner that flowed. And if I couldn't start, I knew I couldn't finish. I thought of beginning with St. John's Revelation but didn't. I tried several entry points along Scripture's epic narrative. I'd ponder and probe, and then back away.

A week passed, then another. Creative concepts swept across my mind, but nothing took hold. Had I raised expectations that could not be met? This kind of second-guessing persisted, with no foreseeable breakthrough.

As time went on, my imagination grew weak; my mind felt soggy. My attempts to spark imagination seemed futile. Words like *fraudulent* and *incompetent* kept pounding in my mind. I became hard on myself, and in a manner quite unlike myself, I considered conceding delusion, offering the brothers an apology.

Yet I knew I couldn't. That would never do. I also knew the Message Makers of Estillyen do not drift into half-hearted acts of message making. We see things through until we've seen them through. That's how we see the things we see. Such thoughts owned me as I paced back and forth in my room.

Then late this afternoon, I knelt in front of my bookcase. I began to read the spines subconsciously, allowing my right index finger to follow along. In that musing sort of state, a thought occurred. I had just touched Tolstoy's spine of *War and Peace*. I paused. I looked to my left; my eyes fell on Fyodor Dostoevsky's *Demons*, and beside it the spine of *Crime and Punishment*.

Next I focused on the row of books above. In the middle of the shelf, alongside *The Collected Works of St. John of the Cross*, I stroked the spine of Victor Hugo's classic, *Les Misérables*. Compulsively I pulled the novels from the bookcase and carried them to my desk. I placed *Les Misérables* on top of *War and Peace*, **then** *Crime and Punishment*, followed by *Demons*.

I sat at my desk, staring at the stack of horizontal spines. I wanted to say something to them, but what does one say to such treasured works? I reflected on the power they possessed. I knew their words; I had read them all.

Impulsively I placed my forehead on the stack and began to recall the redemptive themes of each work. As I rested the full weight of my head on the hefty volumes, all fretting began to melt from my mind. I thought about human worth and the characters captured inside these pages, and the four characters who created them. In that moment the works spoke to me, as a testament of worth.

A strange idea struck me; I wanted to weigh the books. Why, I didn't know. Perhaps I sensed that in doing so, I would find a way size up the work awaiting me. Thus, before I could dismiss the idea, I curled my left arm around the volumes and stepped out the door. I felt inspired in a way, as though I shared in the worth I carried.

I hurriedly moved down the back stairs leading to the dining hall and kitchen. As I expected, I found the corridor to the kitchen empty, and the kitchen too. No one works in the kitchen on Sunday.

I pressed through the kitchen door, clicked on the overhead lights, and headed straight for the scale on the pastry table. The white enamel scale, with its elongated copper pan, outdates most everything in the kitchen.

I reached under the bench, pulled out the stool, and set the books upon it. Next I opened the top drawer, reached for the wax paper, and tore off a strip. I laid the paper in the copper pan and then carefully placed the four volumes inside. I looked at the weights and selected one identified as "5 lbs." I placed the weight on the plate opposite the books, but pan full of books did not budge.

As a result, I added a pound, followed by another. Still the pan did not rise. The third pound added to the five affected the rise. The books went up swiftly, forcing the weights to fall with a hammering thud upon the white porcelain base. I had found my range of weight: more than seven pounds and less than eight.

This called for smaller weights. I started with a weight marked "8 oz." At that point the scales began to teeter. I laid my finger on the weights and, with the slightest touch, achieved balance. Therefore I added a small one-ounce unit to the stack of weights, which, in turn, balanced the books. In all, the four books weighed seven pounds nine ounces.

Then I weighed them one by one. The hardback copy of *Les Misérables* weighed in at two pounds nine ounces. It outweighed the soft cover edition of *War and Peace* by two ounces. Dostoevsky's *Demons* and *Crime and*

Punishment, both soft cover editions, topped the scales at one pound ten ounces and one pound four ounces respectively.

With the weighing exercise completed, I put everything in order. I shut off the lights and made a hasty exit for my room. I trusted that my act of weighing classic works would remain an act unknown to all but me.

Back in my room, I set the books on my desk and began to peruse them, looking for highlighted lines, scribbled words and phrases. I always leave a trail of markings through books I prize. The extent of scribbled lines, notes, and marks attests to the worth I attach to the work.

Anyway, I turned first to *War and Peace.* I knew the lines I wanted to find. A single line, or even a phrase, can draw me right back into the heart of the narrative. I found the little lines on page 1055. A line above them I read first: "Petya began to close his eyes and rock." Then followed the little lines: "Drops dripped. Quiet talk went on. Horses neighed and scuffled. Someone snored."[24]

There, in the middle of war, peace. I can live on such lines, carry them with me for days. Not just for the sentiment conveyed, but for their brevity and for Tolstoy's brilliance in weaving them into the narrative. Great works live on; they do not die.

I inspected several other highlighted lines in *War And Peace,* but after a while I put down the weighty novel and picked up *Demons.* A couple of yellow sticky notes protruded from pages near the end of the novel. They directed me to the final chapter, titled "The Last Peregrination of Stepan Trofimovich."

On the spread of pages 652–653, highlighted texts and underlining appeared profusely. Instantly I entered into the narrative, recalling how Stepan Trofimovich had fallen ill in the remote town of Ustyeov. Confined to bed with feverous chills, the eccentric poet and philosopher pleads with a bookseller named Sofya to read him selections from the Russian New Testament.

The yellow sticky notes had drawn me to the precise text I wanted to examine. Sofya had just read the Sermon on the Mount to Stepan Trofimovich as he lay listening with rapt attention. Eventually he said, "Enough."

I continued reading the lines on which my eyes had fixed. He said to Sofya:

"My friend, I've been lying all my life. Even when I was telling the truth. I never spoke for the truth, but only for myself, I knew that before, but only now do I see. . . . Oh, where are those friends whom I have insulted with my friendship all my life? Enough, enough, my child, perhaps I'm lying now; certainly I'm also lying now. The worst is that I believe myself when I lie. The most difficult thing in life is to live and not lie . . ."[25]

Indeed, I held in my hand a weighty work, first published in 1872. I thought, "Worth of words not fading into time. Such works tap eternal themes, and so live on." As I closed *Demons* and placed it on the desk, a question pressed upon my mind. "What value might I contribute to a novel slim?"

I picked up *Crime and Punishment*, and immediately turned to the passage I knew I would. On page 420, the young prostitute Sonya confronts the young murderer Raskolnikov. She tells him, "Go now, this minute, stand in the crossroads, bow down, and first kiss the earth you've defiled, then bow to the whole world, on all four sides, and say aloud to everyone: 'I have killed!' Then God will send you life again."[26]

At that point my mind felt full. I wanted to ponder everything. I sensed my spirit moving with direction, even though my mind had yet to see the light. So I restacked the novels, placing *Les Misérables* on bottom of the pile. Symmetrically *War and Peace*, proceeded *Demons* and *Crime and Punishment*, ended up on top.

I sat down and once again stared at the spines. I thought, "Lord, more than a million words lie bound before me. I've weighed them, seven pounds nine ounces in all. The weight sounds like a newborn statistic. I pray, not for a pound or two, but for a few ounces that bear the weight of what I desire to write."

I smiled; I felt comfort within. A line from Jesus' transfiguration leapt into my mind. "Get up; don't be afraid," Christ said. I thought, "The disciples, too, saw a vision they could not immediately reconcile. Yet they didn't flee. They stayed in the narrative and lived out the story."

To the stack in front of me, I resolved do the same. Intuitively I felt the novel would somehow emerge out of the other sphere. I thought, "I didn't invent the vision; it arrived. Or, better still, I arrived in it." So I prayed, not well, not articulate, but I prayed.

In due course I made my way to bed, where I tossed and turned. Words and lines swirled about my mind. I kept thinking of bread—I suppose due to the weighing exercise at the pastry table. In my mind I could smell bread. I kept thinking about kneading dough and how yeast makes the dough rise. I drew a parallel to words kneaded into a narrative, how the story grows.

Though late, I felt compelled to get up to see if I could capture some of those words on paper. My mind had already begun to reconcile phrases and fragments together. I got up and stepped to the window in the narrow cove. The cove's cloistered space offers its own reassuring sphere. The composition of plaster, wood, and stone does not define it. Something slightly transcendent abides in the space, long ago constructed.

Standing before the window in the cove, I shut my eyes and allowed the stilling sphere to quiet me. I breathed, softly, silently. After a half minute or so, I opened my eyes and peered down at the pools of light lining the cobblestone street. Instinctively I reached for the brass window latch and pulled the sash open partway. Cool air raced past me to fill the room.

Again I closed my eyes, but amazingly the pools of light did not disappear. In my mind's eye, I saw them, as clear as sight can render. Hesitantly, I opened my eyes, but the vision continued.

To my astonishment, I saw the elderly man with a cane standing in the farthest ring of light. As before, he beckoned me to enter. I did—while still standing in the cove. I beheld not a dream, but a world in which my double existed.

I saw myself, as me, acting distinct from me. The otherworld me knew nothing about my third-person observation from the cove. The vision flowed in one direction, not two. He existed in the other world as first-person me, Narrative.

I felt compassion for the soul of my other self. On his own he operated, thought, and talked. I had no idea what he would do. But I knew this strange experience had everything to do with the story I longed to tell—namely, the depth of redemption's story . . . though I had no idea how this might come about.

I believed the answer would soon present itself. So I closed the window and latched it. With that, the vision ceased, though life in the other sphere continued. I knew it did so, just as heaven carries on despite the deeds done on earth.

Monday started briskly, with early morning prayers and Mass. Breakfast, chores, and rounds at the infirmary followed. From there the duties of the day unfolded, producing no noteworthy surprises. My anticipation rested on the hours following dinner, when, in my room, I would see what the mind's eye could see.

A simple dinner of goulash and yeast rolls aided my quick exit from the dining hall. According to my watch, I reached my room at quarter past seven. Into the door, I inserted my key, turned the knob, and entered. I had a goal in mind.

Swiftly I cleared my desk and placed it in the cove. The small oak desk fit perfectly, with an inch or so of clearance on either side. The back of the desk pressed flush against the wall, about three inches beneath the descending windowsill. The window itself sat deep within the trim-less sill.

Next I gathered my pens, pencils, and clips and slid them into the desk drawer. On top of the desk, I placed a single pen and pad, along with my lamp. Its green porcelain shade provided perfect light without reflecting into the window.

Darkness soon moved the twilight along. With everything settled, I un-latched the window and took my seat. Instantly, the backdrop of Port Estil-lyen captured my thoughts, my being. A gentle breeze flowed in, carrying the scent of pine. Slowly I drew the scent into my nostrils.

Darkness pressed in to hover near the alluring luminous rings. I closed my eyes momentarily and then opened them to the world beyond. Instantly I recalled words penned by St. Paul. I could hear the words, as if the apostle stood next to me speaking them. I wanted to look at them literally, though, so I stepped over to the bookcase and quickly located the passage in the sacred text.

"I knew a man in Christ above fourteen years ago (whether in the body, I cannot tell; or whether out of the body, I cannot tell: God knoweth); such

a one caught up to the third heaven. And I knew such a man, (whether in the body, or out of the body, I cannot tell: God knoweth), how that he was caught up into paradise, and heard unspeakable words, which it is not lawful for a man to utter."[27]

Moving back to the desk, I thought, "St. Paul did not ascend to paradise with a quill in hand." No definitely not. He must have absorbed the experience, seeing sights, hearing things, which he, by heaven's edict, could not share. The otherworld experience, I decided, belonged to the one experiencing it, not the one watching it.

Rather than composing a novel from the cove, I concluded, the other me would have to bear the responsibility for my novel conviction. He, after all, not me, ran through the luminous rings in search of the man with a cane.

Scary thought, though, to place my hopes in the other me. Would his otherworld experience lead him, and therefore me, down the road of redemption where we needed to go? My hunch said yes; my mind could not agree. Faith and trust I had, and nothing more.

Each evening, I took my place beneath the window in the cove to silently observe myself in the drama. I determined to stay prayerfully near, believing the two of us would somehow come out of this together.

Only then, would the story present itself as mine to tell. Until such point I'd watch my other me carry on, in a world he knew but didn't know. "Poor fellow soul," I thought. I suppose I landed him in this mystery, when a mere novel did not miraculously materialize, with the nettle grasped.

In this regard, Ellul had influenced me. I recalled words of his I had come to use in my ministry. "Today Communication has been broken because the intellectual is no longer 'neighbor' to anyone. He is no longer understood by other men because he no longer has anything in common with them."[28]

I felt confident my other me would find neighbors, in his world beyond the luminous rings.

PART TWO
Surreal Life of the Other Me

CHAPTER FOUR
All Saints and the Mysterious Visitors from Afar

At precisely noon, I found myself standing under the tower clock on Pearl Street without a clue how I got there. Dressed in casual attire, I clutched a small, brown leather suitcase in my right hand. I immediately thought, "Why did I decide to shed my habit?" Mystified, I looked at my suitcase and concluded I must have packed it—but why?

Since taking my vows, I've never donned casual clothes in public, except when camping or fishing. The getup, though, allowed me to move about incognito. But why would I want to go around incognito? My process of thinking baffled me as much as my attire.

Yet my faculties functioned, as did my senses. Rather like someone who has fainted coming to, sights, sounds, and words roused my state of consciousness. In that moment of awakening, a snap decision lodged in my mind. I decided to drop by All Saints Church and visit Fr. McVinch. I hadn't seen the wise old priestly priest for more than a year.

Visits with Fr. McVinch had always lifted my soul. I knew of no one better able to access a peculiar incident than Fr. McVinch. He lives among peculiar incidents—thrives on them, I believe.

So I continued along Pearl Street, darting in and out of fast-paced pedestrians. My path took me to the corner of Main and Shore, in the East End. All Saints has occupied that corner for nearly two hundred years. The church enjoys a landmark status in Port Estillyen. With the Estillyen fete in full swing, I assumed I'd find Fr. McVinch at the church. The church has sponsored fete-related events for decades.

In less than twenty minutes, I reached All Saints and quickly ascended its worn granite steps. I had climbed those steps so many times before; I felt the steps knew me by my feet. At any rate, I set down my suitcase and started to ring the bell, when the door opened. Congenial Dennis appeared.

Before I could say hello, my friend Dennis said, "Hi, my name is Glynnis, welcome, come right in, we've been expecting you. So glad you saw the ad; right this way. Sorry, I'm on a call. Just go on into the library and make yourself comfortable. I'll just be a minute."

I stepped through the door, and Dennis, claiming to be Glynnis, swiftly disappeared.

"What?" I thought, as my mind rattled with dissonance. Glynnis for Dennis, and he greeted me not joking. I began to perspire. I felt faint, frightened. I didn't know which way to turn. Reality had gone; everything felt out of kilter. Perhaps my hearing ratcheted words in some obscure manner. I needed to get a grip on myself, settle, think.

I nervously stepped across the hall and into the library. I began to force upon myself thoughts of normality.

"Yes, I'm here," I said.

"Where?" I asked.

"You know," I said, "All Saints Library staring at theology works and selections on communications theory."

"And the reason for the latter?" I asked.

"I know," I said. "That dates to the nineteenth century, when former newspaperman Benton Harlow entered the clergy."

"I can think, process," I said.

"Okay, stop it," I told myself. "I'm not in danger; exist, settle, just wait. I'm alive."

I listened to myself and whispered the word *contemplate*, followed by the word *calm*. Obeying my whisper, I breathed thoughtfully. I glanced up at the plaster wall above the library entrance. A line of hand-painted calligraphy read:

My words will never pass away.
–Jesus Christ, the Nazarene, son of Mary, Son of God

I let myself admire the delicate lettering, black outlined in gold. Alone in the library, I saw rows of spines, but my mind couldn't take in the titles. My thoughts churned within my maelstrom of insanity. I decided to step back into the hall just as Dennis reappeared.

"Yes, as I mentioned, my name is Glynnis," he said. "And yours?"

"I thought you would recognize me—I'm Narrative," I said. "Of course, you've never seen me without my habit."

"I see you now, but I don't recall seeing you before," Glynnis said. "But that doesn't matter. I'm sure you'll do a great job in sorting the books. What a mess!"

I dismissed the comment and simply asked, "Is Fr. McVinch in?"

"Fr. McVinch?" Glynnis asked. "No McVinch here. You must mean Fr. McQuince. Amazing how people twist that name."

"No, I've spoken correctly—Fr. McVinch," I said.

"Well, you may have spoken correctly," he said, "but sorry to say, you're incorrect. Only one father here for the past thirty-five years, and McQuince is he."

I started to reply when he said, "Oh, I forgot, the meeting. I'll be back in less than an hour. Please get familiar with the library—what a mess. Make yourself at home. I'm off."

Off he went. The hall fell quiet. I stepped back into the library and noticed a small, wood-framed mirror on the end of bookcase nearest the entrance. I needed to see myself. Perhaps I didn't exist, as me. Though I definitely wanted see me reflected in the mirror. I even thought I might not be real, in this space surreal.

I looked straight into the mirror. I peered deep into my eyes. They belonged to me, clearly. Still I felt my intestines gnarled. I looked away, and then peered again. I watched myself watching myself, stupefied.

I thought, "Books, Scripture, literature—I must read something. Can I read? Can I comprehend?" I needed to place my mind in something literal. I need a reservoir for my insanity, a text I knew.

Just beyond the mirror I looked upon a row of As—works aligned by authors. Feeling nearly desperate, my eyes quickly fell upon the spine of *Anselm*. Along the length of the spine I read *Anselm of Canterbury: The Major*

Works. "Perfect," I reckoned. I knew the volume well, and what could offer greater mooring than a text stretching back a thousand years?

I plucked the volume from the row and headed to the huge round wooden table in the center of the library. I recalled sitting there on several occasions, both for meetings and by myself. Two dozen oak chairs surrounded the table. With no one in the library, the empty chairs and empty table welcomed me with solitude. I scooted into the chair nearest me and opened *Anselm of Canterbury* to a random page. I preferred randomness, hoping for a bit of existential enlightenment touched with transcendence.

I laid the book on the table in front me, allowing the binding to flop open at sections pre-cracked by other readers. My portion opened to the spread on pages 208–209, in the chapter titled "On the Fall of the Devil." My eyes landed on a pencil-marked segment on page 208.

Therefore, although no one says that nothing is something, but we are always driven to say that nothing is nothing, still no one can deny that the word *nothing* is significant. But if this noun does not signify nothing but something, what it signifies seems to be something and not nothing.[29]

I had fallen into the text of the Student, not the Teacher. I turned the page to glance at a few lines from the Teacher.

But that which is only an absence of reality is certainly not real. Hence evil in truth is nothing and nothing is not real, and yet in a way evil and nothing are something because we speak of them as if they were real . . .[30]

"No, insane," I murmured. "If I had my own copy . . . I know the gems of Anselm, but not now, searching . . . . What next?"

I set the volume aside and headed back to the As, praying my way along. Scripture verses kept revolving in my mind. "Thou will keep him in perfect peace whose mind is stayed on thee, because he trusteth in thee . . . . I know the plans I have for you . . ."

Not far from a second copy of Anselm, I saw the perfect work—*Confessions* by St. Augustine. I hastily grabbed the classic and beat a path back to the table. I quickly thumbed through the well-worn work until I came to Book Seven, knowing the richness that it contained. I found the text at the bottom of page 106, still yearning for a spark from on high to arrest me. I began to read:

I now believe that is was your pleasure that I should fall upon these books before I studied your scriptures, in order that it might be impressed on my memory how I was affected by them; and then afterward, when I was subdued by your scriptures and when my wounds were touched by your healing fingers, I might discern and distinguish what a difference there is between presumption and confession—between those who saw where they were to go even if they did not see the way, and the way which leads, not only to the observing, but also the inhabiting of the blessed country.[31]

Leafing back a few pages, I placed my eyes on another section with lines and pencil-marked slashes.

And I entered, and with the eye of my soul . . . above my mind the immutable light. It was not the common light, which all flesh can see; nor was it simply a greater one of the same sort, as if the light of day were to grow brighter and brighter, and flood all space. It was not like that light, but different, very different from all earthly light whatever. Nor was it above my mind in the same way as oil is above water, or heaven above earth, but it was higher, because it made me, and I was below it, because I was made by it. He who knows the truth knows the light, and he who knows it knows eternity. [32]

In my reeling state of insanity, I knew I had just reckoned with wisdom and comprehended its pattern flowing. A sense of comfort beyond understanding seeped into my soul. I determined I would face my disorientation tethered to hope.

I closed *Confessions* and stilled myself in the quiet of the room. A few minutes passed in that stilling time. Then footsteps I heard. Down the hall at first, but steadily they neared. Soon the sound of a clearing throat let me know the steps had arrived. Into the library doorway stepped the man calling himself Glynnis. He looked down the main aisle and spotted me.

"There you are," he said, as he entered the library and walked in my direction. "Good, good, oh, a bit of study I see. Used to be very busy, this library. Anyway, so it is in this modern digital age."

I stood and started to reply, when three sharp strikes on the front door ceased our conversation. Officially rapid and strong the strikes had beat upon the door. Quizzically, Glynnis looked at me, and I at him. He said, "Pardon me; please wait." He turned and headed toward the door.

I moved over to an inconspicuous spot where I could view the front door without detection. Glynnis hurriedly opened the door and said, "Hello."

In the center of the doorframe stood a man the likes of which I had never seen. He wore knee-high black leather boots, baggy trousers, and a long auburn waistcoat. His white shirt sported a double row of silver buttons that slanted inwards from the top and extended to his waist.

The man had a warm smile that complemented his kind features and penetrating blue eyes. In his right hand, he clutched a slender dark cane with a silver handle. His outfit was quintessential seventeenth century.

"Greetings, my good man," he said to Glynnis. "Your promptness commends you. I've come to call on the priest, Fr. McQuince. I trust he's in?"

"As it happens, he is," said Glynnis. "Yet your visit does not appear upon the calendar, correct?"

"It could be construed that way," the man said.

"As you would understand," Glynnis said, "time does not allow Fr. McQuince to receive impromptu calls. I surmise you must be part of the fete."

"Yes, we aspire to play a part in the fete," said the gentleman.

"Your name for starters," Glynnis asked. "And have you traveled far? That makes a difference to Fr. McQuince. Locals nearby can re-jig their schedules and circle back around."

"Yes, certainly, I understand. Once we resided near, but on this occasion we've traveled quite far. My name is Bevin Roberts. I'm here with my troupe of four. We're the Message Makers of Old."

"Hmm . . . very much in character, I see," Glynnis said. "Well, I'll check; do step in. I can't promise you anything, you know. I'll check."

Utterly stunned, I peered on from the library. Glynnis stepped back, allowing Bevin Roberts and his troupe to enter. Then he closed the door, made a circuit around the guests, and headed off. Briskly he made his way down the long, terra-cotta tiled hall toward the study.

My heart pounded. I began to tremble. I placed my knuckled left index finger between my teeth and bit down firmly, holding the bite. Anxiety seized me. I started perspiring again. I felt faint.

The word *hallucination* floated through my mind. "No," I thought, "a person hallucinating can't analyze their own experience. Or can they?"

Just then, I heard the sound of footsteps and muffled conversation coming up the hall. "A respite of reality," I thought. "In a matter of seconds, I'll see Fr. McVinch. Clarity will wash away this madness."

I trained my eyes on the narthex. The footsteps halted as two men stepped into the light beneath the massive wrought-iron chandelier.

"Well, hello there! My name is Fr. McQuince," said the elderly priest, extending his hand to Bevin Roberts. "Glynnis tells me you have traveled far."

"Yes, quite true, Fr. McQuince," said Bevin Roberts. "It's a privilege to meet you. Do forgive the abrupt nature of our visit. Please allow me to introduce my troupe." He looked beside him and said, "Brother Oracle is here on my right, and next to him is Inquisitor. On my left we have Voice, followed by Sojourner."

I watched in total disbelief. I trembled but felt paralyzed to act. I didn't know what to do, except breathe and listen.

"Yes, pleased to meet you," said Fr. McQuince, as he moved along the line shaking hands with the troupe. The troupe wore more casual attire than Mr. Roberts, but of the same period. Their jackets fit loosely, with rounded shoulders and single button cuffs. Their boots appeared to be made of soft, pliable leather.

"Fr. McQuince, if I might," Bevin Roberts said, "I'd like to address our station here. It came to our attention that certain peddlers of disquiet have come to the Isle of Estillyen to bark against the tenets of truth. In fact, we passed them along the high street this very day."

"You don't say," said Fr. McQuince.

"Not that we are against fetes, Your Eminence," Roberts said. "Certainly not—in fact, we're most fond of them. Yet during fetes, insurgents often filter in spawning distressing messages. We've witnessed the phenomenon in some of the most cherished villages and hamlets. A word here linked to a phrase there can form lines that mold grievous messages. With hate they hack away at truth, condemning praise."

"You don't say; I think I know what you mean," Fr. McQuince said.

"Yet the matter is not trivial," Roberts said. "Attractive and alternative messages stretch back as far as the ides of Eve. We've come to offer message making of another ilk, dramatic readings based on Scripture narratives. May the efficacy of your prayers find fruit in our endeavorers? This hope we lay before you."

"I see," said Fr. McQuince. "And these readings you mention, do they have a theme, perhaps a title?"

"Certainly, Father," Bevin Roberts said. "The theme and title are one and the same: 'Divine Choreography of Redemption.' We wish we could offer a week of readings, but we'll have to slice it up due to other commitments. With your good wishes, we would commit to three afternoon matinees. After that, we must depart."

"Slice, you say?" Fr. McQuince replied.

"Yes, we'd prefer late afternoon matinees—Monday, Wednesday, and Friday—that's how we'd like to slice it. We have another engagement in a destination rather far from here, but nearer now than before, since we are here. We'll spend a week preparing, but following the Friday matinee, we'll need to be on our way."

"I see, albeit, a bit further," said Fr. McQuince. "Redemption—I'd like to hear more, but not here in the narthex. The aroma in the air calls to me. There's a fresh apple crumble in the kitchen. I'm confident that crumble can find its way to the dining hall in the company of tea. That is, if you care to join me. We can slice it up as you please."

Bevin Roberts smiled and said, "We'd be honored . . . delighted, Father." The troupe uttered not a word, but simply grinned and nodded in unison. A look of cheer swept across the unique mix of faces. Fr. McQuince began to lead the way, as fast-paced Glynnis disappeared ahead of the guests.

Awestruck, I watched Bevin Roberts stroll down the hall with Fr. McQuince. The priest walked with a priestly gait, occasionally adding in a sideways, swaying sort of step. It's a technique that makes priests appear spiritually drawn, rather than self-propelled.

I thought, "How can I ever begin to rectify what I've just witnessed? I know above my shoulders I have a head, with eyes and ears, but they can neither reconcile nor reject the madness in my mind."

Soon the narthex and hall fell silent. My impulse, once again, turned to the small mirror on the end of the bookcase. In slow motion, I moved toward it, until my face pressed to within a few inches of the glass. I cocked my head to the left, giving my right eye prominence in the mirror.

The forced closeness to my image gave me a rush of madness, which I welcomed. I felt no shame in probing my probable insanity. In fact, the notion of insanity seemed to offer a solution to my surreal existence. I thought, "Surely, I must teeter upon the precipice of delirium."

Still staring into the mirror, I offered myself a slight smile, and then another. I reflected upon Fr. McVinch who had somehow become Fr. McQuince. "How could anything elicit more confusion?" I questioned. Certainly, Fr. McQuince looked like McVinch, walked and talked like him, but he claimed a different surname, making him a different priest.

As into the mirror I continued peering, a voice behind me spoke without warning.

"Good, you're here." The voice belonged to Glynnis.

I spun around and said, "Hi."

"Is everything all right?" Glynnis said.

"Yes," I said. "Perfect."

"I'm afraid I'll have to show you to your room and then carry on," Glynnis said. "Supper is in the dining hall at six o'clock, and breakfast in the morning at seven. I'll plan to join you for breakfast, and afterwards we'll meet here to discuss the library. I'm thrilled the library will soon be sorted. Shall I help you with your case?"

"No, no," I said.

"By the way," he said, "please feel free to take along the books you were reading."

"Sure," I said. I quickly made my way back to the round table and picked up *Confessions* and Anselm's volume. With the two works in my hands, I approached Glynnis more like a discarnate soul than a man.

"OK, right this way," Glynnis said.

Together down the terracotta hall we walked, side by side. When the door to my room shut, I sat on the edge of the narrow bed, pensively. On the wall a small, simple wooden cross hung. The cross looked totally out of proportion to the wall's height and width. I stared at the small object intently.

A thought struck me that had never struck me. "When Christ emptied himself to become man, as St. Paul put it, not considering 'equality with God something to be grasped,' what precisely did he empty?"

The line of thinking, I knew, had something to do with me, with my state. Compelled, I pondered on. "Incarnate, God became man, yet God abided fully in the man. His words speak of this duality in one, do they not? 'And he said unto them, Ye are from beneath; I am from above: ye are of this world; I am not of this world.'"

The train of thought I could not shake. I asked myself, "In emptying himself did he suffer pangs of emptiness? In that gasping, dying hour of abandonment, surely he did so. Does he know my emptiness?" I wondered.

Words from the Book of Hebrews answered me. "For we have not a high priest which cannot be touched with the feeling of our infirmities; but was in all points tempted like as we are, yet without sin."

In the chamber, a sea of whys pressed in upon me. I wondered, "Why these thoughts beyond me, at such an hour and place I do not know? Yet I know the truth of this simple cross."

Occasionally I'd rise and pace about, only to promptly sit back down. Everything raced to-and-fro in my mind. Eventually I stretched out on the bed, turned on my side, and dozed off.

After a while, I awoke to a darkened room. The darkness didn't frighten me. I clicked on the table lamp beside my bed and picked up *Anselm of Canterbury*. In the light, I navigated freely through the text. Soon I found words that captivated me:

> Do you not understand that, supposing any other person were to rescue man from eternal death, man would rightly be judged his bondslave? For man . . . would be the bondslave of someone who was not God and to whom the angels were not in bondage.[33]

I closed the book. I savored the words. Still, I wanted to flee. But where would I go, and how would I get there? I thought of King David, who feigned insanity to escape detection from his enemy. I grinned as I considered the incident—how he pounded his head on a city gate and let spit drool from his beard.

As the night passed and with it ensuing days, I toyed with this sort of ruse. I considered muteness. I realized, of course, nothing like that would do. I knew my identity, even if no one else did. A solution of sorts came to me. I'd simply exist, hour-by-hour, and from there, day-to-day. Thus in this mode I continued, trying to comprehend what I couldn't understand.

When probed by Glynnis about my residence, I simply said I'd been on a long pilgrimage and had stayed at the monastery for some time. As soon as I'd start to elaborate on matters of reality, he'd surface a topic that would spare me.

Regarding the library post, Glynnis had spoken over the phone to someone named Nate about the temporary assignment. Nate was supposed to show, but didn't. Glynnis obviously took me for Nate. I planned to depart if Nate arrived. In the meantime I began to catalogue books, sorting titles and authors and clearing out redundancies.

I felt like a spy, a madman, moving about the corridors and rooms of All Saints. How else could I feel after what I'd seen and heard? Bevin Roberts, who founded Estillyen's Order of Message Makers, had arrived. Bevin Roberts and his troupe once again walked the streets of Port Estillyen.

"No big deal," I told myself. "Just enter another sphere, as angels tend to do." I resolved simply to live, to go on breathing, eating, and sleeping. I coached myself to be vigilant, to watch and listen, to take copious notes, to be a dutiful scribe.

Subsequently I learned much from Glynnis. He recounted details of the afternoon tea with Bevin Roberts, Fr. McQuince, and the troupe. Glynnis discovered, to his amazement, that Roberts knew nearly everything about the comings and goings of Port Estillyen.

In particular, Roberts knew that All Saints had acquired Theatre Portesque a few years ago and renamed it Anselm Hall. He also knew about the ongoing renovation effort.

According to Glynnis, three groups had vigorously competed to book the venue for the duration of the current fete. Two groups eventually bowed out, as the renovation work kept missing deadlines. A third party remained a viable option until news arrived that the upholstery shop's warehouse had burned to the ground. Four hundred and eighty six newly upholstered theater seats went up in flames.

All Saints, therefore, had no takers on booking a freshly painted, seat-less Anselm Hall. The mysterious arrival of Bevin Roberts, however, changed the picture. Apparently, the venue featured prominently in Roberts' conversation with Fr. McQuince.

Roberts contended that Anselm Hall would be ideal for the troupe's dramatic readings. "No seats, no problem," Roberts said. "We'll scatter about and round up benches, boxes, stools, and chairs." Roberts claimed the eclectic seating would enhance the atmosphere of the readings.

As time progressed, my concentration moved solely to Bevin Roberts and his troupe. What would they make of the theme "Divine Choreography of Redemption"?

"How will it go?" I wondered. "Will I be positive, and, if not, what then? A negative experience would prove devastating, for me personally and for the Order of Estillyen Message Makers." All such thoughts troubled me.

Yet I had a new identity. Promptly nicknamed "Nat" by Fr. McQuince, Nat attached to me as naturally as a button on a collar. And anyway, *Nat* possessed two-thirds of *Nar*, with only a two-letter skip from *r* to *t*. So Nat suited me, except when summoned, as in "Hey Nat." Somehow, then the little noun sounded more like "bat."

However, these bits and pieces of daily routine didn't possess me. The whole mirage, in which I existed as Nat, held me in a trance. Odd upon odd the atmosphere seemed, and more so than that. I moved about spellbound, wondering if I'd suddenly blink my eyes and be me again, forgetting all that had taken place.

No matter what, I determined I would face disorientation tethered to hope.

CHAPTER FIVE
Seeing Redemption

The intimate Theatre Portesque had enjoyed a strong public drawing on Front Street for 111 years. Then one day, to everyone's shock, a pronounced crack suddenly appeared on the face of the structure. The ominous crack resembled a jagged lightning bolt extending from the foundation to the roofline.

Some locals, a minority, called the incident an omen sent by providence against theatrical performances. The theory gained a bit more steam the following week when a portion of plaster mask fell from the right cheek of Tragedy. The plaster landed on the theater's stone steps and shattered into powdery pieces.

The main advocate behind the omen theory scooped up the shattered pieces and carried them around in a string-tied pouch. He presented his gleanings, to anyone who would listen, as a kind of indisputable artifact. Despite the speculation, investigators soon unearthed the reason for the structural damage. Water from a broken pipe had swirled away a sizable amount of dirt, causing Portesque's foundation to shift.

After a while the crack widened to such an extent that pigeons and other birds began to perch along the crevice. The nests, made of twigs and straw, added even greater complexity to the building's face. In time the Safety Department stepped in and tacked a notice upon the front entrance that read: "Closed by order of Public Health and Safety." Estillyenites mourned the theater's closing.

During the three-year stretch that followed, all manner of schemes emerged to try and save the historic site. Several investors announced plans, but they all fizzled. Despite well-intentioned efforts, the reality of demolition loomed. It seemed certain that a future sidewalk plaque would mark the site where the beloved Theatre Portesque once stood.

Events came to a head a couple of years ago when, early on a Monday morning, Muller & Sons hauled in its huge blue crane and unloaded it in front of the theater. A sense of dread spread through the community. Workers posted warning signs reading, "Danger—No Parking—No Pedestrians."

The signs spoke of demise; everyone knew that the following day Muller's wrecking ball would swing through the facade of old Portesque and destroy the interior. Estillyenites expected bricks, balusters, and beams to fall into a massive, dusty heap tangled with wires and chunks of plaster.

Except the expected did not occur; the swinging ball never swung. One might say a miracle occurred. An anonymous benefactor who had recently sold a field used the money to purchase Portesque. To everyone's surprise, the unknown gentleman immediately bequeathed the property to All Saints Church. Further, the private soul added a tidy sum for renovations.

Word circulated that the veil of anonymity shielded a wealthy Catholic with a passion for the arts. The benefactor's attorney remained mum about the generous mystery person. However, once someone overheard the attorney say, "Catholics are good at keeping secrets." Since he, too, professed the Catholic faith, no one knew for sure what he meant.

All in all, it took All Saints more than two years to convert the site into a multiuse venue. In the process, Theatre Portesque acquired a new name, Anselm Hall, in honor of Anselmo d'Aosta, archbishop of Canterbury from 1093 to 1109. Even so, most Port Estillyen residents still call the venue the Portesque.

Adjacent to Anselm Hall, a narrow, two-story structure houses Pastry 45. According to public records, a pastry shop has occupied 45 Front Street since the day the building opened. Pastry 45 uses the front half of the long, narrow brick building, and All Saints uses the remainder of the building, including the entire upstairs, for storage.

At one time a twin structure abutted 45 Front Street and extended to within an arm's length of All Saints Church. A well-used footpath ran between the church and the former building. In an expansion phase, All Saints acquired the twin structure and tore it down.

The church converted part of the space into a key garden with a wrought iron fence running along the sidewalk on Front Street. This morning I acquired the key from Glynnis and entered the garden just shy of three o'clock. I brought along a book to fill the time prior to the four o'clock matinee. I found an empty bench near the side wall of 45, where I watched people already beginning to mill around Anselm Hall.

Over the past week, I had read compulsively. Strangely, a few volumes I had read before I speedily reread backwards this time around. I discovered the exercise especially helpful in rereading McLuhan's *Understanding Media*. Previously I had found it very challenging to tackle McLuhan with a logical, sequential approach. Most readers find themselves outsmarted when reading McLuhan. He quickly sprints into matters of complexity and diversity and never breaks his stride.

The backwards method, however, allowed me to sneak up on various key points and topics. The topics seemed to lay open on the page, unguarded by text arranged to meet the reader advancing along the prescribed course. As I read, I reverted to the old-school method of penning notes and quotes on cards. I used to practice this approach routinely, and I frequently used the cards as bookmarks.

Seated on the garden bench, I opened Ellul's *Humiliation of the Word*. One of my note cards, containing a McLuhan quote, marked the place. I thought, "Funny to read these fellows here, in my state of mind." Yet their words meant more now, than ever. I had found the volumes huddled together in the library; they showed considerable wear.

The quote on the card read: "Just as we now try to control atom-bomb fallout, so we will one day try to control media fallout."[34] I could hear McLuhan speaking, or so it seemed.

I flipped over the card, not realizing I had penned a second McLuhan quote. It read: "It is one of the ironies of Western man that he has never felt any concern about invention as a threat to his way of life."[35]

I reflected of the platform builder and the discarnate man. I could hear

Discarnate speaking, as well, saying, "Repeat after me that charming noun aiding discarnate life: *algorithms.*"

Next I scanned the page open in front of me. Penciled checkmarks, not mine, drew me to Ellul's lines. "People refer continually to sight as the ultimate criterion, but it is blind to ultimate things. The *seeing of invisible things* . . . is a new dimension in sight. Sight becomes true when it proceeds from or is transformed by faith."[36]

I sat pondering the relationship of faith-induced sight. I thought about how screens project selected, fragmented reality. I asked myself, "We need more prophets speaking out about fallout with alarm concerning the global state of media ecology?"

I wanted to read on, but I stopped. My mood shifted; I felt too absorbed in anticipation for the matinee. I closed the book, rose from the bench, and exited the garden. I moved along the brick walkway connecting the church to number 45. An arched corridor extended right through the middle of 45, creating a continuous passage from All Saints to Anselm Hall.

Inside the arched corridor, selected art adorned the walls. Midway along the corridor, a striking saying of Jesus Christ predominately appeared:

> My words are not my own.
> –Jesus Christ of Nazareth

The cursive black letters, painted on the white plaster, extended some two meters from side to side. The uneven plaster, bonded tight to the brick wall, added a curvy depth to the lettering. Three lights beamed down from above, making the saying hard to overlook for anyone passing by.

According to my watch, I stepped in front of Christ's words at 3:20 p.m. Rather than entering from the front, I wanted to slip in from the All Saints entrance and occupy an inconspicuous place near the back of the hall. I had intentionally stayed clear of Anselm Hall all week, as the troupe busily arranged the venue.

At the end of the corridor, three swinging wood doors opened to the hall. The red painted doors had sizeable porthole windows with silver metal bands. I cautiously pressed through the swinging door on the right and entered the hall.

Instead of neat rows of cascading theater seats, all sorts of mismatched chairs, stools, planks, and benches decked the hall. Old ladder-back chairs, wooden dining chairs, one-of-a-kind chairs, short and tall chairs, outcast chairs, and chipped and nicked chairs filled the hall's interior.

Young, not so young, and older people busily jostled about, swapping seats and settling into place. The crowd mingled naturally, rather joyfully, as if they'd been doing so for years. Smiles, kind gestures, and nods animated the hall. Before long, all the seats were taken. Several young people stood, leaning against the walls on the outer aisles.

I found a seat in the back, not far from the porthole doors. I recognized a number of people—at least I thought I did—but no one recognized me. Every familiar face turned out to be someone slightly askew, like Fr. McQuince for Fr. McVinch. Oddly, hair color caught my attention. In particular, I noted red-haired people dotted about the room, amidst heads blonde, black, and shades of gray. Bald heads conspicuously appeared here and there.

To my left, four college-age young ladies occupied chairs of variable heights.

"Hello," I said to the young lady nearest me, while extending a smile to the rest. The young lady replied, "Hi, my name is Doris; we're from St. Angus College in Century."

"I know it well," I said. "My name's Nat."

I immediately thought, "I just lied, I think. Why did I put forward Nat, rather than Narrative or Nar?" The puzzlement erased my smile, and I settled back into my seat.

At precisely 4:00 p.m., Fr. McQuince stepped out onstage. "Welcome, friends, to Anselm Hall, former home of the historic Theatre Portesque. My name is Fr. McQuince. So very pleased to see you—we didn't know if anyone would show. From what I can tell, every seat, box, and bench appears occupied.

"Yes, let me say on that score, we're very sorry about the temporary seating. As many of you know, the original theater seats were lost in the recent fire at Finches' Upholstery. Such a blaze—not a single seat was salvaged. Anyhow, it's courageous of you to make do and offer yourselves in a merry mood.

"Today's reading will commence minus the choir. Once again, accept my apologies. Tomorrow we'll have the singers not present today. Seems the choir from St. Angus missed the Estillyen Ferry. However, as you can see by the cameras dotted about, the media team made it. I understand they'll transmit the proceedings to the mainland in some fashion or another.

"Now, concerning the Message Makers of old, I'm not sure how to introduce them. That's because I've only recently met them, and I have never actually heard them. This chain of events came about in twinkling of an eye, so to speak.

"I can say this for the troupe: they certainly stay in character. It's as if they dropped in from another planet. Not so, though—they have a small clipper ship, just offshore, moored in the far side of the mist. Sounds peaceful, doesn't it?

"So, without further ado, it's my pleasure to welcome Bevin Roberts and his troupe to Anselm Hall." As Fr. McQuince exited stage right, the tall red curtain slowly closed. The audience watched as the motorized hum brought together the large gold-embossed A and H insignia.

With the curtain closed, Bevin Roberts and his troupe entered through a small side curtain near the front of the stage. They proceeded single file and stepped down onto a secondary stage covering the orchestra pit. Unlike the straight stage above, the lower stage had three semicircles that protruding into the audience.

Bevin Roberts made his way to the center semicircle, which extended further into the audience than the other two. The troupe fanned out to semicircles left and right, where they promptly sat down on tall wooden stools. With everyone positioned, Roberts began to speak.

"Good afternoon. My name is Bevin Roberts. Thank you for attending. We're truly heartened by the turnout. We consider it an immense privilege to be here in Port Estillyen. Port Estillyen is one of a kind in a world of ports."

I thought, "Indeed, Bevin Roberts."

Roberts continued, "I'm joined this afternoon by my troupe. To my right, I present Brothers Oracle and Inquisitor. On my left we have Voice, followed by Sojourner. As you can readily see, the red velvet curtain behind us is drawn. You may be wondering why we're not up there rather than here. Simple: if we were not down here amongst you, we would be on stage without you, and near is where we desire to be.

"With that said, I'd like to say a brief word about our overarching theme: divine choreography of redemption. The triple nouns *divine, choreography,* and *redemption* act in unison when brought together. The words *divine* and *choreography* speak of how *redemption* came to be, how it became a feat of historical reality. This theme challenges us to think holistically about the Holy Writ's source and its raison d'etre.

"Yes, yes, you must peer equally *at* and *through* the lines of the Holy Writ to grasp the full meaning, even though you never will. Peering *at* the lines, you find the words stitched together in the context of culture and time. Probe them, pick them, and chew upon them as the prophet Jeremiah did. Yet beware; let not the literal sense bar you from the deeper sense.

"'Now faith is the assurance of things hoped for, the conviction of things not seen.' A visible line of Holy Writ, it is speaking of things invisible. That's the way the lines work. Limit not the heart's perception to the naked eye's reception.

"Yes, yes, I know you know that words matter. Words have the power to mold and make us, heal and harm us. They can also help redeem us. Whether spoken, written, or signed, the words we profess confess the measure of our faith.

"So, I ask you, have you paused to ponder the makeup of words? Not just their prescribed meaning, but how words emerge and abide? Words bear thoughts in alphabetical apparel. Words turn the mind inside out.

"The high priest, in the order of Melchizedek, spoke precisely of cornering the power and promise of words. You'll find one of the most astonishing lines on the wall in the passageway leading to All Saints. Read it. Ponder it. No one else, in all of human history, ever testified, 'My words are not my own.'"

I, like everyone else, sat riveted, listening to the figure on the stage. Then he paused, and without cue or prompt, Oracle rose from his stool, took a single step forward, and into the silence spoke: "When the fullness of the time had come, God sent forth his Son, made of a woman . . . to redeem those under the law, that we might receive the adoption of sons."

Forcefully yet rhythmically, Roberts continued. "The words *fullness of time* speak of time ticking, do they not? If so, who sets the clock and then watches it as it ticks and tocks present days away? Grain by grain, sand particles fall through heaven's unseen hourglass. Yes, Scripture draws us back in time, allowing us to ponder those seminal acts of time filling."

As I listened my real-world worries tamped down and I felt strangely welcomed by the surreal world in Anselm Hall.

"Enter the ancient text where you wish. However, halt not at the words set out upon the lines. See through them. With the mind's eyes, look backstage at Scripture's making. There you will see God at work, making moves, keeping time, watching the clock from eternity.

"Let us consider, too, words of Shakespeare. You know them, no doubt. 'All the world's a stage, and all the men and women merely players; they have their exits and their entrances.'[37]

"Yes, yes, stage right and left we enter. We play our parts; we speak our lines. We linger awhile, with voices fading, and then, in time, we ebb away. Never can we stay beyond our allotted days. We go, as surely as we came. To the wings we exit. God goes with us, but just as surely stays. The immovable one sees the drama through. He forgets not the parts we play, nor the reason we acted out the day.

"Oracle, into this train of thought, please speak."

As before, Oracle rose and said, "For the prophecy came not in olden times by the will of man, but holy men of God spoke as they were moved by the Holy Ghost."

"Speaking of God," Roberts said, "what a bold thought St. Peter sets forth. Yet, he speaks to the heart of divine choreography. Not a fragment here stitched to a patch there. No, no, not at all; the spine of Scripture is divinely stitched with the golden thread of redemption.

"Yes, yes, it is so! Just as a modern day philosopher has said, the Holy Writ 'seizes ultimate mystery from all angles, and in so doing, revels truth itself.'[38] How can it be that the Word made flesh spoke not words his own? Yes, yes, no, no, we can't probe that line fully just now. That we mustn't do, no, no. Yes, that we mustn't do.

"Today's reading, if a reading it is, is titled 'Seeing Redemption.' I ask you, how does one see redemption? As you see, I have no script to aid me in saying what it is I want to say. We need a story—yes, yes, a story to tell."

"I happen to have one," Inquisitor said as he rose from his stool.

"It must be a very special story," Roberts said, "for we are in a very special place, Anselm Hall."

"Yes, that I know," Inquisitor said. "Did I not travel with you to this wondrous place?"

"Surely you did," Roberts said. "This story of yours, Inquisitor, it's not a fairy tale, I hope."

"No, no, nothing of that sort," Inquisitor said.

"Good! Please tell it then," Roberts said.

"No, no, I didn't say I'd tell it—only that I have it," Inquisitor replied.

"So how do we hear it, if you will not tell it?" Roberts asked. "What about giving the story to Voice, so he can tell it?"

"I would, but I actually got it from him," Inquisitor said. "So I can't give him what he already has."

"Patience, I beg you; please do not desert me," Roberts said. "Voice, do you know the story of which we speak?"

"Certainly," he said.

"Pray tell, Voice, tell it well," Roberts said.

"Yes, though I must have you know that it's an expansive tale," Voice said.

"Fair enough," Roberts said, "as long as you shorten it."

"I'll try," Voice said.

"And it relates to our theme, right?" Roberts asked.

"Certainly it does," Voice said. "It even speaks about names written in heaven. Shall I tell it, then?"

Roberts did not reply verbally, but turned and looked at Voice with a pose rather stern.

Voice stepped into the middle of the semicircle stage left, and began to address audience.

"The story is not mine, only mine to tell. It comes from the narrative of St. Luke, the physician who wrote Theophilus to offer an orderly account of Jesus Christ's ministry on earth. St. Luke assured Theophilus that he had investigated everything quite thoroughly.

"Shortly following the Transfiguration, in Luke's narrative, the author inserted the story of Jesus sending out the seventy-two. Luke placed it just prior to the parable of the Good Samaritan.

"At any rate, Jesus Christ sent the seventy-two on their way. It's on this occasion that Jesus said, 'The harvest is plentiful, but the workers are few.' Which he followed with a single word command—'Go!' He then proceeded to tell them, 'Behold, I send you out as lambs amidst the wolves.' Sheep amidst wolves, he instructed them not to take a purse, a satchel, or even sandals.

"Now to the point, of what they were to do. Jesus told them to heal the sick and declare, 'The kingdom of God has come near to you.' He went on to say that if their message was rejected, they should go into the streets of that particular town and say, 'Even the dust of your town that clings to our feet, we wipe off against you.'

"Jesus added, 'I tell you, on that day it will be more tolerable for Sodom than for that town.' This he also said, 'He who hears you, hears me, and he who rejects you rejects me, and he who rejects me rejects him who sent me.'

"So, like lambs they went, and among wolves the disciples said what they said and did what they did. In time the seventy-two returned. They spoke not a word about dust or rejecters rejecting. Quite the contrary, the seventy-two returned rejoicing. They said, 'Lord, even the demons are subject to us in your name!'

"In response, Jesus Christ said, 'Nevertheless do not rejoice in this, that the spirits are subject to you; but rejoice that your names are written in heaven.' Then, he offered a most startling confession. Jesus said, 'I saw Satan fall like lightning from heaven.'

"'Tis a matter to ponder," Voice said. "Sir Roberts, shall I leave the story at this stage, or offer another word or two?"

In a calm voice, Roberts said, "Both. That is, kindly repeat the line about rightly rejoicing. Then leave the story at this stage, so we can pick it up again later."

"Yes," Voice said. "The line as you wish is, 'Nevertheless do not rejoice in this, that the spirits are subject to you; but rejoice that your names are written in heaven.'"

As Voice returned to his stool beside Sojourner, Roberts stilled his frame but not his eyes. Never have I seen a man stare so intensely. Into a sphere beyond he seemed to peer. His striking countenance gripped the crowd. Then he continued, speaking now with a voice more buoyant and rhythmic.

"Words and phrases first, meaning next," Roberts said. "*Harvest plentiful, workers few, kingdom near, midst wolves, lambs sending, Go! no, no purse, no sandals, peace resting, tell heal, dust clinging, hearing rejecting, Satan falling, lightening heaven, demons submitting, disciples rejoicing, names written . . .*

"Oh Theophilus, simply a passage in Luke's letter to you, what did you think when you read those incredible words?

"Oracle, read the prayer Jesus Christ's offered just after saying 'names written.'"

Oracle stepped forward stage right, clutching a very thick, leather-bound copy of the sacred text. From St. Luke he read:

In that hour Jesus rejoiced in spirit, and said, I thank thee, O Father, Lord of heaven and earth, that thou hast hid these things from the wise and prudent, and hast revealed them unto babes: even so, Father; for so it seemed good in thy sight.

All things are delivered to me of my Father: and no man knoweth who the Son is, but the Father; and who the Father is, but the Son, and he to whom the Son will reveal him.

And he turned him unto his disciples, and said privately, Blessed are the eyes which see the things that ye see: For I tell you, that many prophets and kings have desired to see those things which ye see, and have not seen them; and to hear those things which ye hear, and have not heard them.

"Theophilus, what are we to make of such telling words ushered from the heart of divinity? You saw them freshly penned. You saw them resting on the parchment, though speaking: *Father Lord, Jesus Son, prophets kings, wise prudent, things hid, eyes blessed, see seen, hear heard . . .*"

The audience clung to Robert's every word; they watched his every move as he carried on a prolonged and fascinating dialogue with the invisible Theophilus. I anxiously wondered what he would do next. Then he stopped.

"So, Sojourner, where would you like to go along the trail of the seventy-two?"

"Me?" Sojourner asked. "Well, I'll go where you wish. In fact, I'll go anywhere—you know me. I must travel. Journey—the very word lifts my soul and readies my constitution."

"What about a journey to hell?" Roberts asked.

"No, well, I mean, you know what I mean, within the narrative of St. Luke," Sojourner said.

"Yes, I agree," Roberts said. "But!"

"But what?" Sojourner asked.

"But in contemplating the words and lines of Holy Writ, it's often beneficial to consider other works that help us fall more freely in to the text."

"Free-falling," Sojourner said. "Falling into the text; that sounds peculiar."

"Would you prefer *plunge deeper*, Sojourner?" Roberts asked.

"Yes, that sounds more adroit," he said.

"OK, plunge or fall, did Jesus Christ not say, 'I saw Satan fall like lightning from heaven'?" Roberts asked. "You needn't answer . . . just come with me."

"Where are we going?" Sojourner asked.

"You said you will go anywhere," Roberts said. "So come close, center stage. Let's go to the unexpected."

As Sojourner moved to join him, Bevin Roberts stepped over to a small chest sitting atop a waist-high wooden table with long slender legs. He opened the chest, lifted out a book, closed the lid, and returned to his spot in the middle semicircle next to Sojourner, who stood to his left. Sojourner glanced over at Roberts with a curious look on his face.

"What do you see, Sojourner?" Roberts asked, as he held the book out for both of them to see.

"A book," Sojourner said.

"Indeed, but not just any book," Roberts said. "I hold in my hand a copy of Dante's *The Divine Comedy*."

"I see," Sojourner said.

"Have you read it?" Roberts asked.

"Not it, but bits of it," Sojourner said.

"Here, read this line, if you have a mind," Roberts said, as he held book open for Sojourner and pointed with his right index finger.

Sojourner read, "'You've seen the door, dead words scribed on its beam.'"

"What door does Dante mean?" Sojourner asked.

"Ah," said Roberts. "The door is a gate, a gate to the City of Dis, as in hell. Would you like to enter, beneath the beam of dead words scribed?"

"I sort of like it here in Anselm Hall," Sojourner said.

"So do I, but Alighieri has gifted us with an allegory that helps one see beyond the optic eye," Roberts said. "Here, let me turn the page and offer you another bit to read. Dante turns his words outward, addressing you and me. Go on, read it to the audience—everyone is listening."

And with a theatrical voice, Sojourner read:

Look hard, all you whose minds are sound and sane,
and wonder at the meaning lying veiled
beyond the curtain of this alien verse.

"What did I just read?" Sojourner asked.

"Dante wants the reader—in this case you—to see beyond the words," Roberts said. "He speaks truth in the form of myth."

"He must have seen a lot, this Dante Alighieri," Sojourner said.

"Glimpse these lines," Roberts said, as he turned another page, "and read them like a poet, true. Still outside gates of the City of Dis, Dante's companion, Virgil, removes his hands from Dante's eyes."

Dutifully Sojourner read:

"And now," he said, "stretch straight
your strings of sight across this age-old scum
to where the fumes are thickest, stinging most."
    Like frogs that glimpse their enemy the snake,
and vanish rapidly across the pond—
diving till eachsits huddling on its bed
    I saw a thousand ruined souls or more

scattering in flight, ahead of one whose pace
passed, yet, kept dry, across the river Styx.[39]

"What did I just read?" Sojourner asked again.

"The ruined souls scattering in flight are the souls in hell," Roberts said.

"I see," said Sojourner. "So who did they glimpse crossing the river Styx that caused them to scatter across the pond?"

"An angel from heaven, who came to open the gates of hell," Roberts said. "Much we cannot do by sheer want and will. With a touch of his rod the gates opened. As Dante said, 'Nothing held them firm.'"

"So the gates did not prevail," Sojourner said.

"No," Roberts said. "Think again about Christ's line spoken to the seventy-two rejoicing. 'I saw Satan fall like lightening from heaven.' Do you think he meant the words allegorically?"

"No," Sojourner said.

"Why not?" Roberts asked.

"Because Satan is real," Sojourner said. He's embedded in the Gospel narratives. In the barren desert he sorely tempted Christ, wanting the Son of God to worship him."

"Right you are, Sojourner. Christ meant what he said. Perhaps he spoke of Satan's original fall from heaven or his spiritual defeat of Satan as the seventy-two cast out demons along the way. Could well be both. I favor one notion over the other."

"Which?" Sojourner asked.

"I'll not tell you, Sojourner. Suffice to say, Jesus Christ did say on another day, 'Before Abraham was, I AM.'

"Listen now to how Dante depicted the ancient foe, as I read, skipping the gory parts of the passage."

With Sojourner watching on, Roberts clasped the novel in both hands and began to read:

And then when we had got still further on,
where now my master chose to show to me
that creature who had once appeared so fair,

he drew away from me and made me stop,
saying: "Now see! Great Dis! Now see the place
where you will need to put on all your strength."

The emperor of all these realms of gloom
stuck from the ice at mid-point on his breast.

How great a wonder it now seemed to me
to see three faces on a single head!

Behind each face there issued two great vanes
all six proportioned to a fowl like this.
I never saw the size in ocean sails.

Not feathered as a bird's wings are, bat-like
and leathery, each fanned away the air,
so their unchanging winds moved out from him,
Cocytus being frozen hard by these.[40]

"Lucifer, Satan, the Evil One, frozen in the river Cocytus, to mid-chest, with bat-like wings whirling the wind that froze him in—this is what Dante saw. Myth, of course, riding on the wings of reality tethered to the realm of divinity.

"So, Sojourner, how did we travel to the City of Dis from sending out the seventy-two?"

"Not sure; I believe that's down to you," Sojourner said.

"Yes, yes, we need to get out of here," Roberts said with a smile. "Let's put *The Divine Comedy* aside, and consider other words more uplifting."

Roberts turned and stepped over to the small chest, carrying *The Divine Comedy*. He opened the round lid, placed *The Divine Comedy* inside, and pulled out a very thin scroll with a blue ribbon tied around it. He gently shut the case and returned to the center of the stage.

"I hear words, once spoken, now speaking," Roberts said. "Not Dante's, but others, not dead upon Dis' door-beam etched, but in my heart attached.

Living and active, they move. They divide the soul from spirit and reckon with heart and mind. They are the version never fading.

"The words now speaking are the words of Christ. They say, 'Blessed are the eyes which see the things that ye see.' How do we see what he told the disciples they saw? This is the question, the seminal question, for all of us. Listen . . . see.

"St. John's words I also hear. 'And the light shineth in darkness; and the darkness comprehended it not.' Light shineth!

"Words from the prophet Isaiah now press upon my mind. 'For since the beginning of the world men have not heard, nor perceived by the ear, neither hath the eye seen, O God, beside thee, what he hath prepared for him that waiteth for him.'

"Yes, yes, so it was until Jesus Christ stepped onto the pages of human history, changing forever its course. Without his appearing, the forerunner dressed in camel's hair would not have been in the desert preaching on the day he saw who he saw. When John the Baptist saw Jesus drawing near, he said, 'Behold, the Lamb of God who taketh away the sin of the world.' Yes, yes, *Lamb behold, sin taketh*. How did John the Baptist see what he saw?"

Roberts turned around and said, "Voice and Inquisitor, please join Sojourner so the audience can see three standing in place of one." The two came forward and joined Sojourner to Roberts' left.

"Now I will affect your fall, for which you are not prepared," Roberts said. "It's simple: when you hear the word *fell*, you *fall*, faces down. Any questions?"

"Yes," Inquisitor said. "This doesn't pertain to Dis, does it?"

"No, quite the opposite," Roberts said. "We've laid down the myth to pick up history replete with mystery. It's here in my hand, a tiny scroll with a small passage, possessing meaning great. Shall I read it?"

"We feel you will no matter what," Voice said.

"I will," Roberts said. "Will you listen well?"

"We will no matter what," Sojourner said.

"Good," Roberts said, as he untied the blue ribbon wrapped around the slender scroll. He slipped the blue ribbon into this pocket and unrolled the scroll. His right hand clutched the top of the scroll, while his left hand held it open.

Roberts turned the scroll to give the three a glance at the text. "See, the words are surrounded by lots of white space," he said. "I like white space."

"Yes, we see," Inquisitor said.

"I like words framed thusly," Roberts said.

"Now listen," he said as he began to read in an eloquent voice:

And after six days Jesus took with him Peter and James and John his brother, and led them up a high mountain apart. And he was transfigured before them, and his face shone like the sun, and his garments became white as light. And behold, there appeared to them Moses and Elijah, talking with him.

And Peter said to Jesus, "Lord, it is well that we are here; if you wish, I will make three booths here, one for you and one for Moses and one for Elijah."

He was still speaking, when lo, a bright cloud overshadowed them, and a voice from the cloud said, "This is my beloved Son, with whom I am well pleased; listen to him."

When the disciples heard this, they fell on their faces, and were filled with awe.

When Roberts spoke the word *fell,* Inquisitor, Sojourner, and Voice dropped down and pressed their noses to the floor, as instructed. Roberts continued.

But Jesus came and touched them, saying, "Rise, and have no fear." And when they lifted up their eyes, they saw no one but Jesus only.

With the passage read, Roberts curled the scroll in his right hand, and used it like a wand to gently tap on the heads of the three lying on the stage. They rose with eyes trained on Roberts.

"Yes, yes, transfigured," Roberts said. "Let us draw treasured nuggets from this small passage in the tiny scroll. Still the scene, frame it in your mind, and ask."

"What?" Inquisitor asked.

"Ask yourselves who orchestrated this phenomenon extraordinaire.

Think of it, as it is truly is an act in the drama divine. *Moses, Elijah, a cloud, a voice, God speaking, Jesus transfigured, garments white, face shining . . .* no false props, but clearly a stage!

"The world and heaven met on the Mount of Transfiguration to play out a pivotal act in the divine choreography of redemption.

"Now, unstill the scene and place yourself within it. Observe. Listen, see what the disciples heard and saw. Extract the most essential acts laced among the lines. Have you grasped them? We must put forth two in our quest of seeing redemption. One follows the other, but we offer them together:

This is my beloved Son . . . listen to him.
When they lifted up their eyes, they saw no one but Jesus.

"Listen! See!

"Dear friends, in closing, we leave with you these lasting thoughts to hear and see:

Harvest plentiful, workers few, kingdom near, midst wolves, lambs sending, Go! no, no purse, no sandals, peace resting, tell heal, dust clinging, hearing rejecting, Satan falling, lightening heaven, demons submitting, disciples rejoicing, names written . . .

"Thank you and good night!"

Bevin Roberts and the troupe took a single bow, waved, and walked through the curtained exit stage right.

Amidst the hall filled with hardy applause, I sat, wondering what I had just seen and heard. The word *amazing* dominated my mind.

CHAPTER SIX
Key Garden with Mr. Kind

I had no compulsion to rush out of Anselm Hall following the striking matinee performance by Bevin Roberts and his troupe. The mood in the hall arrested me, pleasingly. A swift departure, I knew, would belie the warm reception evident on the faces in the hall.

In fact, following Bevin Roberts' closing lines, no one in the audience sprang to their feet. Instead people tended to meander about. Several individuals congregated near the stage. Some touched it; others tapped on it, as if registering their presence at the event. The crowd seemed to attach an air of importance to what had transpired.

I curiously watched Fr. McQuince, who had gone over to inspect the curtained exit the troupe passed through as they departed the stage. Fr. Mc-Quince kept pulling back the curtain, as if he expected his newly acquired friends reappear. At one point he passed through the curtain, only to return as quickly as he'd entered. Eventually Glynnis came along, and they chatted for a bit, then exited the curtained passage together.

I overheard one gentleman sitting behind me say, "After today Anselm Hall will never be the same." Indeed, the performance had an air that transcended the hall. While addressing the crowd, Roberts and the troupe seemed to also attend to unseen masses. They moved about graciously, mysteriously, in a timeless mode. Though Roberts spoke dramatically, his every gesture flowed from an ardent passion void of pretense.

Eventually the crowd began to thin, filtering through the exits and onto the street. Outside, eager conversation ensued. I mingled about, listening to what people had to say.

"What a surprise!" said a smartly dressed lady, standing in a group of six.

"I thought it would be a thirty-minute do," commented the man opposite her.

"It was truly magnificent," said the slender miss beside him. "Don't you think?" she asked, turning to me.

I couldn't say what I dared not say, reveal what I knew—no one would believe me. So I simply said, "Yes, superb."

"I know," said a tall, thin man in the same huddle. "Who wrote their lines?"

"They're actors, aren't they?" another person asked.

As I strolled through the crowd, I repeatedly heard people ask similar questions: Where did they come from? How did they get here? Where did they go?

Before long, fisherman Charley James appeared, all worked up, at the edge of the crowd. I drew closer and could hear him carrying on about the troupe—how they got in a wooden rowboat down at the harbor inlet and promptly rowed away.

"I seen 'em," Charley said. "The lead fellow, the prominent one with the blue eyes, he sat erect in the bow of the boat, straight as a mast. The troupe faced him, bent over their oars. The oars was long for the size of the boat. All at once, they dropped their oars into the water and began rowing, whilst they hummed some tune I'd never heard.

"Strange sight I saw. They sort of scooted across the surface of the water without pressing into it normal-like. Effortlessly they moved. Sure enough, I'm telling you. They rowed straight toward the mist. And none of 'em said a word. Not a peep—just humming. The lead fellow never batted an eye.

"I watched them close, not taking my eyes off of them for a second. Ever so mysteriously they rowed, sort of eerie-like, but calming too. The whole atmosphere seemed to hush in their presence. In no time, they entered the mist and were out of sight."

Upon hearing Charley's account, several people dismissed it. I overheard a portly fellow say, "Just ole Charley, spinning another tale after a pint or two." Just the same, I knew he spoke the truth. In the company of everyone, I alone knew the troupe's true identity. Yet how can truth abide in the realm of the impossible? Both their appearance and my trance certainly lived in that realm.

Everything roundabout me seemed so mystically strange. While standing there amidst the crowd, listening to comments ebb and flow, a somber mood came over me. The somberness penetrated my mind. The mood centered on the person of Bevin Roberts. I desperately wanted to speak with him directly, tell him what I knew. But how and when would I do so?

As the crowd began to dissipate, I didn't want to go straight back to All Saints. Instead I ventured over to the key garden next to Pastry 45. I adored the quiet grounds. I headed back to the old wooden bench I had discovered under a chestnut tree near the center of garden. There, perfectly alone, I took my seat.

I felt comforted somehow by the bench's tall back and long sturdy arms. I began to ponder the twists and turns of my otherworld fate. After a few minutes, I leaned back, closed my eyes, and forgot about time and place. In a little while I nodded off—not soundly, only faintly.

In the midst of the peaceful quiet, I heard a voice say, "Hello." Without lifting my head from the bench, I opened my right eye. In front of me stood a slim, elderly man, with white hair and a gentle face. He wore a nicely contoured straw hat and held a slender cane.

I quickly opened both my eyes, straightened my posture, and said, "Hello, sir."

"Would you mind if I share your bench?" the gentleman said.

"Please, join me," I said, as I scooted to bench's arm.

"Thank you," he said, as he sat down on my right, placing a small basket between us. The basket had a woven top, which reminded me of my fishing basket. I'd never seen one quite like it.

"By the way, my name's Narrative," I said. "But nowadays I'm known as Nat. I'm doing some temporary work in the church library, sorting out the collection."

Removing his hat, he said, "Pleased to meet you; my name is Mr. Kind." His striking head of white hair didn't have a strand of contrasting color.

"Did you attend the Anselm Hall matinee?" I asked.

"Well, well, yes, in a manner of speaking," he said. "Fine orators, those Message Makers of old."

My attention peaked. What did he mean by saying, "In a manner of speaking"?

"Mr. Kind," I said. "Why does that name ring a bell? We've never met, have we?"

"No," he said, "not to my knowledge."

"Mr. Kind, Mr. Kind . . . I've heard that name, I'm sure of it," I said.

"Well, I'm sure you have, but it's not the sort of name you hear every day," he said.

"Mr. Kind, yes, now I remember. Hollie and Goodwin Macbreeze spoke about meeting a Mr. Kind in Century. They turned their Estillyen venture into a novel, released a couple of years ago. I reviewed the manuscript. That's it; I knew I had heard the name."

"Good on you, my friend," said Mr. Kind. "At least that's off your mind."

"However," I said, "the Mr. Kind described by the Hollie and Goodwin sounded more like an angel than an actual person."

"Do you remember the description of this angel?" Mr. Kind asked.

"As I recall, he was thin with white hair, sported a cane and . . ."

Instantly my senses froze in a way that frightened me. I fell silent. I doubted my hearing, my vision. I didn't know what to say. I interlaced my fingers, reversed my palms, and stretched out my arms. I felt awkward.

I couldn't disappear or evaporate. I rubbed the palm of my hand on the bench's arm. The coarse wood grain assured me of reality, but I felt ill-prepared to entertain a visitor from on high. Truly I had entered a thin space along the lines of some Celtic experience.

Remaining silent, I looked down at the basket and examined it with a studious pose. Slowly I lifted my head and peered into the face of Mr. Kind. His green eyes sparkled and possessed a mystical depth, which I can only describe as purity. Somehow my sense of fear and anxiety vanished.

"This can't occur," I said. "Not here, not now. You see, I'm not in reality—that's altogether real. I'm here, but in a sphere which brought me here.

You're real, aren't you? You have a cane and carry a basket. I've never heard of an angel sporting a cane."

Mr. Kind smiled and said, "A seraph I knew once carried a burning coal with a pair of tongs. Quite a common practice, I must say. However, this particular incident found a place of prominence in the ancient scrolls. By that I mean Scripture.

"Ole Isaiah—just thinking of him makes me smile. What a dedicated soul, that species of prophet. Burning coals to the lips, all the elements brought together by divine choreography, as I like to say."

"Sir . . . Mr. Kind . . . please," I said. "Please . . . I mean I'm caught up in something way beyond me. Honestly, tell me, what's happening to me? If this mysterious state brings much more to bear, I may not survive."

"Do you think you'll die? Do you wish to die, as Job wished?" asked Mr. Kind.

"I don't know," I said. "Please, hear me; I'm swimming in a bizarre existence. I don't want to lose my way, drift away. I'm coping in a world I know, but nothing fits. All the true inhabitants have become characters. I know them; they don't know me. Soon, I fear, I'll not know myself."

"Do you?" asked Mr. Kind.

"Do I what?" I asked.

"Do you know yourself?" he said.

"I thought I did," I replied.

Mr. Kind said, "How do you suppose Isaiah felt when he peered into heaven and saw six-winged seraphs flying to and fro round the throne of God? You know the passage well; I know you do.

"In the presence of the Almighty, the celestial sixers cover their eyes with a pair of wings and their feet with another. With the final pair they fly. Isaiah heard them calling out, saying 'Holy, holy, holy is the Lord of hosts; the whole earth is full of his glory.' The doorposts and thresholds trembled, and smoke filled the temple.

"Isaiah, too, was afraid. And what did he say?"

"'I am ruined,'" I replied.

"Was he ruined?" Mr. Kind asked.

"No," I said.

"Narrative, don't be afraid. Don't doubt the vision of your mind's eye. I'm here not by chance. The same goes for Bevin Roberts and his troupe."

"So you know everything about what I know?" I asked. "I mean, what I'm experiencing?"

"Only what I'm allowed to know," he said. "However, I'm quite familiar with the Estillyen Message Makers."

"What a relief," I said. Then I thought to myself, "I'm mad, surely. I'm sitting under a chestnut tree, talking with a white-haired angel named Mr. Kind. Dear God, what has become of me?"

"Narrative, soon I must hasten away," Mr. Kind said. "But I'll return before your experience is through. What I have to say is important, so please listen.

"So right you are to press into the matter of redemption's divine choreography—though you'll never plumb the depths of acts divine. Pursue your course as if mining diamonds or gold. Take hold of Isaiah's words:

'I have swept away your transgressions like a cloud,
and your sins like mist; return to me, for I have redeemed you.'

"However, beware of adept adaptors who twist and spin the truth of meaning great. Antagonists press against you. Like chameleons they blend in; they broker falsity as a natural trait. Morphing along from one generation to the next, they decry and deride divine intervention. Yet they know not the one 'in whom are hidden all the treasures of wisdom and knowledge.'

"To what you already know, Narrative, there's more you need to know. The day after tomorrow, you'll hear Bevin Roberts and his troupe speak about Lucifer's crime against humanity. Although you know the texts, listen well. The high street fallacy will not go untouched.

"Further, you must speak with Bevin Roberts, converse with him. If you try and avoid him, he'll seek you out. Speak to him about the prize you strain to possess. This is not the time to change the road you're on. Like St. Paul, long for his appearing. Press on . . ."

"Sorry, Mr. Kind, my mind is reeling . . ."

"Worry not," he said. "All will go well, exceedingly so, unless you . . . Looks like rain—see the clouds in the western sky, just over your shoulder?"

When I looked to the west, I saw a wall of dark clouds forming on the horizon. "You're right," I said; "it looks threatening. I wonder if . . ."

I turned back, and Mr. Kind had gone.

"What's happening to me?" I thought. "A thin place, beyond reality, I might as well be on the far side of the moon. I need to see myself, in a mirror, know that I exist."

I looked again to the sky, seeing that shafts of light now breached the darkened wall. I started to get up, when I noticed Mr. Kind's basket on the bench. It felt strange having access to such an object. I stared at it, as one would do when examining a priceless artifact.

I thought, "It appears as real as the bench." Using both hands, I gently took hold of the basket. I placed it on my lap, allowing the leather shoulder strap to dangle down past my knees. By the weight, I knew the basket held something inside. What sort of something, I wondered.

Using my right thumb and index finger, I pulled the tightly pressed wooden peg out of its leather loop. With peg released, the lid sprang open a crack. I tried to peer in, but saw nothing. With my thumbs, I steadily raised the lid. Three items I counted inside. I raised the lid until it swung fully open and slapped flat against the back of the basket.

To my surprise, the unmistakable aroma of fresh-baked bread rose from the basket. A loaf of bread, with salt crystals on top, lay across the bottom of the basket. The height and thickness of the loaf appeared proportionally equal. It resembled a brick paver.

I reached in, and amazingly, the loaf felt warm. Not merely warm, but oven warm, even slightly hot. I lifted it very gently. Carefully, I set the loaf on my lap in front of the basket. I reached in again, extracting one of the two remaining items. This time, instead of touching something warm, I took hold of something cold and damp.

I lifted out a short round jar, full of chilled water. The round top lid reminded me of an Orthodox Church dome. Ribbed lines swirled around the jar, rising up to the gold-colored lid. Cautiously I opened it. I watched as little ripples flowed from the center across the jar's interior expanse. After thirty seconds, or so, the ripples ceased; the water stilled.

Gingerly I placed the jar to my nose and sniffed. A scent, akin to a fresh mountain stream, emanated from the little jar. Cool, too, so much so that the jar dripped a trail of drops, as I lifted it out and placed it on the bench.

One article remained. Against the back of the basket rested an item, flat and thin. As I lifted it free, a streak of light flashed across my face. Into a small mirror I peered. The hazy little mirror had a wooden frame, painted blue. The paint had crackled long ago. I felt a slip of paper on the back of the mirror, which suddenly detached and fell back into the basket.

I reached for the slip of paper, and discovered it bore a personal note. The note read:

Dear Narrative,

Fear not, my friend; be of good cheer. With seeking souls I do abide. When earnest knocking God hears, he lingers near.

Life is a journey, long, not bereft of mystery. Surely you would not wish it otherwise. Though through a mirror dimly you presently peer, be not dismayed; clarity will surely dawn.

Exist in your state of multiplicity until the multiplicity no longer exists.

In the words of St. Paul: "For now we see through a glass, darkly; but then face to face: now I know in part; but then shall I know even as also I am known."

Carry on; the course of life awaits you.

The bread and water I brought for you. Enjoy—question not their origin. More anon,

Mr. Kind

P.S.—Oh yes, once upon a time I coached a learned soul under the cover of night. On that darkened night, he asked the figure of light how a man "can be born again."

Know this: I shall make equal time for you.

CHAPTER SEVEN
Strange Brew — Bewilderment and the High Street Three

I stayed in the garden for a good hour, mulling over the visit with Mr. Kind. Especially his line, "Exist in your state of multiplicity until the multiplicity no longer exists." I found hope in the words "no longer."

Nevertheless, a maelstrom of impressions swirled about my mind. Images and words intermingled, swapping places between the here-and-now and beyond. I had to keep reminding myself of my position. I had entered a world beyond where the surreal mimics life for real. No one can prepare for such an experience.

Eventually I locked the garden gate and went back to All Saints, where I preceded down the hall to the kitchen. As I entered, I greeted Mary Connelly, who stood at the preparation table, busily slicing green and red peppers destined for a salad of mixed greens.

"Hello, Nat," Mary said. "Did you make it to Anselm? I wanted to go, but time slipped away. Fr. McQuince and the others have been buzzing about it. Said the actors did a fine job. So glad the Portesque has been brought back to life—abandoned theaters are spooky. Cobwebs in stalls once filled with laughter and tears . . . I believe spirits of the departed inhabit such places. I do, really."

"Yes, so do I," I said.

"You do? Didn't think you would," Mary said, "given you seem to be so grounded in your faith and all."

"Yes, grounded," I said.

"Who are they anyway, the Roberts fellow and his team?" Mary asked. "I hear they're from Century."

"Yeah, I think you're right," I said. "They're rather mysterious."

I thought, "If I could only tell her which century."

"Their readings are every other day, right?" Mary asked.

"Yes, they're not on tomorrow, then back Wednesday," I said. "They only have two more performances."

"Want something to eat?" Mary asked.

"No thanks, I have a loaf of bread in the basket," I replied.

"Where'd you get it, 45?" she asked.

"Very close," I said.

"There's a wedge of blue cheese on the table," Mary said. "I left it out—I like it better that way—and there's butter too."

Mary and I spent the next three quarters of an hour chatting about food, All Saints, the fete, God, providence, theatre, and the annoyance of flies. In my state of multiplicity, I spoke as Nat, not Narrative, and allowed myself to enjoy the conversation.

The following day I spent in the library, sorting material amongst the M, N, O, and Ps. Wednesday morning I made my way over to Fields and Crops for a cup of coffee. Just before eight, I entered my familiar haunt, only to find it unfamiliar. Like everywhere I turned, it appeared the same, but not.

It seemed like close relatives of the previous owners now ran the place—though more than close, nearly identical, except for notable variations. I recognized a patron who used to have brown eyes; they now had turned green and his hair from gray to red. Likewise, the pace of gaits had changed. Cynthia, a slow-walking waitress I knew quite well, now walked very briskly, while Jake, the limping dishwasher, no longer limped—but Ruth, the cashier, who had never limped, did.

"Table for one?" Cynthia asked.

I simply shook off all that I saw, and answered, "Yes, just one." She seated me near the bow window in the back—a delightful spot for watching the waves roll in upon the Estillyen shore. I had claimed the spot many times before.

"Hi, yes, Cynthia, I just want coffee," I told the miss upon her return.

"Sure, I'll bring it right out," she said. "Black, right?"

"Right," I said.

My coffee arrived in Crop's classic ware, a white cup and saucer with matching rings of green. In that moment I found peace, or perhaps peace found me. But the moment, as moments do, soon expired.

The mood shifted when in walked the three high street profiteers, followed by a tall, sinister-looking figure with deep pockmarks dotted across his face. The tall fellow had a low, rumbling cough, which he buried deep within his chest. The ominous group wasted no time in taking their seats.

Cynthia seated the high street three at a round table in front of the bow window. They sat with their backs to the sea. The sinister fellow sat opposite them. In turn, I sat at the booth nearest the four. I could easily look into the faces of the three, and I had a profile view of the disturbing fellow. I watched curiously as the waitress came back to take their order.

"Yes, hello again, what can I get you?" Cynthia asked.

"Coffee and toast," said one of the three.

"Same for me," said the one in the middle of the window. The third ordered only tea.

"And, sir, what would you like?" Cynthia asked the ominous figure.

He rumbled a cough and said, "A triple espresso in a large mug, and add in all the coffee grinds it takes to make it. Just dump them in on the espresso. Then add some boiling water to the brew. And on the side, bring me a cereal bowl full of lemon rinds. I'll pay for the lemons, don't worry."

"Oh, well, different, but as you wish," she said, and then dashed away.

The three backing the sea looked rather jittery and serious. Due to the contour of the window, I could hear every word spoken.

"OK," said the sinister one. "I'm often called Bew, but you will call me Mr. Bewilderment. I will do most of the speaking, so listen and listen well. Let me get this straight—which one of you is Platform?"

"That's me," said the one sitting directly across from Bewilderment.

"OK," Bewilderment said. "Then I've sorted you two—you are Discarnate," he said to the one seated to the left of Platform. "And you must be Rejection."

They nodded and both answered with a single word. "Right, right," they said.

"So, I see you three are who you are. Know this, I'm not here by accident . . . quite the contrary. I've been summoned, sent. Steady yourselves for what I'm about to divulge. Listen carefully.

"Long I have existed. I am Bewilderment, from the order of Balaam. I am a noun, the spirit of disturbance. A defying demeanor I possess, drawn from within and all manner of matter roundabout.

"Any questions so far?" Bewilderment asked the three, who sat with eyes open wide. "I didn't think so."

In awe I sat. In dreams or life, no scene matched the scene I watched. Nervously I looked up at the ceiling, down at the floor, and across the room. All the while, like sonic waves, words resonated from the bow window, alighting on my ears. Even whispers I easily captured.

"A sketch I import to you," Bewilderment said. "I say *sketch* deliberately because that's all you'll ever get in this earthly sphere.

"Human sphere—that brings me to your near-death experiences. Surprised by my discursive shift? The avalanche put you under, didn't it, Rejection?

"Shush, she's back," Bewilderment said.

"Here you are, gents," said waitress Cynthia.

Into the conclave she stretched, first setting down the cup of tea for Rejection. Next she graciously handed off the orders of coffee with toast, after which she slowly lowered the large dark brown mug of espresso and grinds. She placed it near Bewilderment's left arm. To the brim of the cup, the steaming mixture rose. Lastly she lifted from her tray a bowl of lemon rinds and placed them in front of Bewilderment. The yellow rinds intermingled in an artistic heap.

"Anything else, gentlemen?" Cynthia asked.

Discarnate and Rejection shook their heads with puckered lips, gesturing no. Platform reached for his tea, while Bewilderment dismissed the question as if never heard. In the uneasy chill, Cynthia scooted away.

"Now, back to the avalanche—as I said, it did you in, right, Rejection?"

"Well, yes . . ." Rejection said.

"Enough . . . don't carry on," Bewilderment said, as he reached out his right hand and snagged a clump of lemon rinds in his long bony fingers. He shoved the entire clump in his mouth and began to chew and chomp mechanically without a pause until he swallowed the bitter mush, which he washed down with a gulp from his mug.

Bewilderment commenced again with a double cough, and said, "Your sailing boat capsized, right, Discarnate? I saw it all—resuscitation, resuscitation, oh, how they pressed. One medic said, 'He's gone.' Another said, 'Wait, hold on.' Don't speak, Discarnate. Too many words we have to press into so little time.

"And you, Platform, a mountain climb too far, right? Thin air, exhaustion, collapse, surely like Discarnate you were as good as dead. In fact, you three all but severed the cord that tethers you to this present sphere. Poor souls!

"In your waning hours, when your pulses slowed and your blood began to make its final rounds, we drew near. We arrived to pull you through. No use for God, you professed, declared so defiantly. Decades-long stiff necks the three of you displayed, and, might I say, delightfully so.

"In that valley of shadowy death, you wailed against the other way and its constricting path. You befriended evil. The pleas of a riotous man availeth much. We heard your cries. Our fiery darts revived you—no shield or armor to hamper us in that moment of spiritual will and tussle.

"Oh, the change in each of you after those revival days—delightful it was, and so evident. Discarnate, you never knew you possessed such powers of spite, now did you? In equal measure, Platform, you discovered your newfound knack for poisoned speech. Where did you get that power to woo the crowds?

"And, not least, Rejection, you found the true joy in being blind and leading the blind. Simpler, in vogue, a minimalist mind not burdened with the malformation of ancient narratives. You swapped who for what and carried on digging for secrets in the soil.

"Wiseman three I now see. Therefore you're in, not out. Unknowingly you have become admired devotees. Doesn't that make you feel good? Hmm?"

Discarnate looked down at his toast and grabbed a bite. Platform raised his coffee cup with the saucer and brought the shaking cup to his lips. Coffee leaped about, spilling down the side of the cup and into the saucer. Rejection nervously dunked his teabag up and down in his mug.

Bewilderment carried on. "There is a certain *who* to whom I must introduce you. He is the master of spite, turning right to wrong to make wrong right. Once I fluffed his wings.

"You shall soon see. Thursday, at five before midnight, you must be prepared to receive the simulcast from the Crimson Cliffs. All you need to do is be prepared to listen. Now, how do you do that?

"Like this. Discarnate will provide three screens, which you will place in the middle of the old market warehouse. The warehouse is located directly behind your staging area on the high street. Bring large screens, as big as you can carry, not little laptop-looking things. Don't fuss with cords; all you need are screens and a spirit of reception.

"No one will be around, save me. The warehouse has been vacant for years. It's just down the slope past the hog pens, where the hogs used to be keept for market. Also, don't worry about electricity or lights. You'll not need either; we operate in the dark.

"All you have to do is pick up your screens and follow me. You'll carry your screens through the dark. Once you get started, don't look back; just march, following me. You have nothing to worry about. At that hour, you're not going to get run over by a tractor or a lorry.

"We'll enter through the wide sliding doors in the back. They'll be unlocked. You'll place your screens on some of the old crates lying around, and use the same for seats. You will be there for precisely one hour. No more. What you shall witness is beyond description. One clue I offer you—initiation.

"Any questions, hmm?" Bewilderment said.

"I mean, I say . . . you know I'm virtually blind," Rejection said.

"No problem. I'll tie a cord around my waist and lead the lot of you through the dark," Bewilderment said. "We'll be strung together, in a single line. Once inside, Rejection, you can scoot your crate right up to the screen, and what you can't see you'll hear. Blindness has its advantages—deafness too.

"Nothing more you have to ask? You must be wondering why the privilege of my visit has been afforded to you. Two primary factors hurried my dispatch.

"First, your efforts of late have not gone unnoticed; especially how you forwarded your messages here in Port Estillyen. You drew in the curious meandering along the high street. All the while, a great hoard of witnesses encircled you from below.

"You, after all, have been entrusted with the great undertaking—that of sowing seeds of discord and rejection. Today the fleshy fields are ripe with easy pickings. No more due season waiting; now is the hour to reap. This is the day of big data,[41] algorithms, and a profusion of words hacking words. It's all so wonderfully confusing for the meaning makers.

"Second, Bevin Roberts and his troupe suddenly materialized from the Estillyen mist. How regrettable, this turn of events. It's not fair—bygone souls appearing from where, a celestial sphere? Same trick pulled with Moses and Elijah on that transfixion day. Everyone else has to bear the weight of the gravitational pull, play within the rules, until the divine sphere grants exception.

"Roberts is dangerous. I thought about you three debating him, but you would only lose. You might storm the stage, though. That is, if you're not frightened to death after you get a peek of the Crimson Cliffs.

"Roberts believes too fervently and sees too perceptibly; that's his problem. He's like the old, repurposed Saul. Once drawn up in celestial mystery, no one could stone the nonsense out of his head. On the matter of preferring life or death, what did he say? I am in 'strait betwixt.' How's that for clarity, reason?

"'Straight betwixt, strait betwixt'—no wonder they carried the madman off to Rome. The Athenian poets pegged him right. In Rome, he sat around in chains. I can imagine him there. 'Strait betwixt, strait betwixt, come listen to me, and I'll tell how your soul gets fixed.'

"Nonsense, all of it, I say. The Master is deeply distressed over the cosmos trajectory. And right he should be. The opposition has skin in the game. The fault line, originating from that old outcrop near Jerusalem, has created a chasm that runs right past the gates of hell. Preposterous! The evil and the wicked have their cosmos rights.

"Anyway, don't let me get sidetracked, or should I say 'straight betwixt?' Say, you look sober, clumps—what's wrong with you nutcases? Soon you'll see how right it is to turn right to wrong, to make wrong right. Besides, it's far too late to change the road you're on. Where do you think you're headed, Emmaus?

"Any final words before we go? Discarnate, call the waitress and pay the bill. My espresso is gone, my rinds too. I'm out of here."

With the bill paid in notes and coins, the strange conclave rose and headed for the door. When Bewilderment passed my booth, he fixed his gaze upon me. Hauntingly he stared, in a momentary pause. I looked down to evade his stare. When I looked up, I saw his back.

The high street three jostled for the door, and once outside, aligned themselves as a passage of outstretched arms. The passage Bewilderment quickly passed.

I closed my eyes for a few seconds in an attempt to rest my maddening mind. Then words fell upon me: "Sir, will that be all?"

"Yes, thanks," I said.

"Never saw the likes of them before," Cynthia said.

"No, nor have I," I said.

"Anyhow, I wish you a pleasant day," she said. And with that, Cynthia whisked away.

CHAPTER EIGHT
Stand at the Crossroads — "Look, Ask, Knock"

The appearance of Bewilderment with the high street three at Fields and Crops deeply tormented me. How could I ever understand what I saw? Wits and reason no longer applied. Had I actually seen bony-fingered Bewilderment scooping coffee grounds from the bottom of his mug? I heard the scraping spoon. I saw the grinds. I watched him chomp and chew.

All the same, I carried on. I departed Fields and Crops shortly after Bewilderment and the three had gone. I stepped out into the Estillyen breeze and began to walk through Ladybug Meadow. On I walked for an hour or more. Pleasing sights and sounds surrounded me, but I couldn't take them in. I found myself increasingly incapable of separating specter from substance. "Erie, frightening, too real, unreal," I thought.

When I returned to All Saints, I heard the phone ringing in the library. I had never heard it ring. I didn't know the black, dial-faced object *could* ring, it appeared so hefty. I stepped over to the refectory table and started to answer it, when the ringing suddenly stopped. I smiled at the silent phone and strangely recalled McLuhan's observation about the tension created by a phone ringing on a stage.[42]

Surely I stood on a stage, in a drama deep. I wanted the phone to ring again, but it didn't. It just sat there, silent, with its horizontal handset resting above a dial displaying numbers worn and indistinct. I wanted to talk with someone, anyone who would listen. But I knew the party on the line had gone. If I picked up the receiver, I knew I would hear nothing but the sound of an empty, mechanical hum.

Instead I moved through a long row of books to a lone wooden chair at the end of a stall. I sat and prayed, thinking, "Lord, why would you allow a mortal like me to see what mortals should not see?" On and on I mused, prayed, and pondered, intermingling and converting thoughts to prayers and prayers to thoughts.

I thought, "The best of souls tire of kneeling, praying, waiting, wanting, holding fast to hope unseen." Yet I did not want to capitulate to sorrow. I had never done so. I knew that I would see through my state of seeing though until I saw what needed to see.[43]

In time, I heard Mary calling down the hall. "Hey Nat, come have some chicken soup with Glynnis." Surprised, I looked at my watch to see that noon had passed a half hour ago. I made my way to the kitchen. Mary's soup offered up an aroma that grounded me. I thought, "The mundane smell of chicken soup—how wonderful."

As the afternoon ensued, I forced myself to quit deciphering every twist and turn of the unknown. I carried on in the library sorting through texts to give away. Still, I couldn't avoid trolling a volume or two in search of a line offering momentary solace. Among the As, I found such a line on page of 128 of Augustine's *Confessions*: "Now, I did not will to do what I willed, and began to will to do what you did will."[44]

I continued on in the library till three. Glynnis and I had decided to attend the matinee together. So at a quarter past three, we made our way to Anselm Hall. At the end of the corridor, we could hear the buzzing of the crowd beyond the red porthole doors.

We entered a packed hall with less than a half-dozen empty seats on the main floor. We made our way to the balcony, where we sat on a plank. I watched people scurrying about, trying to claim a spot or squeeze in here and there.

Out of the corner of my left eye, I suddenly saw something move. A head had popped through one of the swinging porthole doors. Swiftly the head withdrew, only to pop through again. A few seconds later, two heads appeared, one above the other. "The lower head," I thought, "must belong to someone on hands and knees, and the upper head to someone leaning on the kneeler."

With the two heads still poking through the doorway, I saw a third head, with bulging eyes, moving back and forth between the triple portholes. The head would appear in one porthole for few seconds, then another. Back and forth the head bobbed, appeared, and disappeared.

Then it struck me: the heads belonged to the high street three. I don't know why I didn't instantly recognize them. The porthole head belonged to Discarnate, and the heads below to Platform and Rejection. All three looked manic. Suddenly the heads disappeared, and a uniformed man stepped through the middle swinging door. His outfit identified him as a traffic warden.

With no seats remaining, people starting moving into the All Saints nave. Given Monday's turnout, Fr. McQuince had recommended setting up an audio link between the hall and the nave, and he ordered signs posted throughout the hall. Glynnis and Les, the church technician, spent most of Tuesday setting up the audio link and posting the signs.

At 4:00 p.m., perfectly on time, Fr. McQuince walked onstage in front of the curtain. "Good afternoon and welcome to Anselm Hall," he said. "I see we have a full house; wonderful. I also know a number of folks have gathered in the nave. So if you can hear there in the nave, welcome, nave listeners.

"I'm disinclined to burden you with announcements. To the extent possible, we've tried to eliminate that practice. Anyway, it makes everything more spontaneous.

"So, I shall simply say that the St. Angus A Capella Choir is ready to sing. Following the choir, the Message Makers of Old will give a reading titled *Stand at the Crossroads–Look, Ask, Knock*. You will want to listen. And, oh, by the way, there will be a short intermission.

"Now let's give the St. Angus A Capella Choir a round of applause."

While Fr. McQuince walked off stage, amidst the applause the stage curtain slowly opened. Eighteen young people stood on two risers. To the left stood nine young ladies, smiling more readily than the young men on the right. The audience focused intently on the director, a slim woman dressed in a black, wearing medium height heels and black stockings.

Suddenly her hands rose, mouths opened, and melodious voices filled Anselm Hall. The performance transformed the restless crowd. Heads stopped twitching, bodies quit squirming, and sideways conversations ceased. The crowd behaved like seasoned concert goers. The half-hour recital quickly passed. The choir opened with "Hear My Prayer, O Lord" and closed with "Deo Gratias."

Bevin Roberts and the troupe could not have hoped for a better atmosphere. As the stage curtain closed and hid the choir, Roberts appeared on the lower stage, with his troupe following close behind him. The troupe members quickly fanned out across the triple-arced stage and took their positions on pre-placed stools. Oracle brought along a portable metal music stand, on which he placed his sacred text.

Roberts found his place in the center of the stage, where he stood still, exhibiting perfect poise. He looked to the balcony, as if inspecting the faces, and then brought his eyes down and scanned the hall from side to side. Then, without any words of introduction, he said, "Let us not tarry as second more. We must go to the crossroads, where we shall ask, look, and knock our way along the ancient drama.

"Inquisitor, Voice, and Sojourner, please join me and station your stools to my left so we can see eye-to-eye."

The three rapidly complied.

"Oracle, kindly come near as well; you have the words we wish to hear."

Oracle came forward, holding open his old, leather-bound copy of the Holy Writ.

"We must have a starting point," Roberts said, "if we intend to get to where we need to go."

"I thought we were already here," Inquisitor said.

"We are," Roberts said, "but we must move on to the crossroads spoken of by the prophet Jeremiah."

"Isn't he the prophet who allegedly ate the words he received from on high?" Voice asked.

"Yes," Roberts said, "Jeremiah claimed such words were 'his joy and heart's delight,' if I have that right.

"Oracle, as you can see," Roberts said, "we have a lot of people watching you and me, in the company of the other three."

"Yes, I know," Oracle said. "I see hundreds of eyes."

"Do you believe the watching eyes are sympathetic to words arising from the Holy Writ?" Roberts asked.

"This I do not know," Oracle said. "Do you?"

"No, only the beholder knows what the beholder knows," Roberts said. "Our role is to speak the words we know, passionately. Yet you can do so with volume, bearing in mind the Christ's words about rooftop shouting."

"I'm not keen on heights," Oracle said. "I'd rather be here, on stage, in the beauty of Anselm Hall. Would you prefer to read the Holy Writ?"

"No, no, please carry on," Roberts said. "The hall of eyes is watching your every move."

Oracle straightened himself, cleared his throat, and said, "The words of the prophet Jeremiah as set out in the Holy Writ."

> *This is what the Lord says:*
> *"Stand at the crossroads and look;*
> *ask for the ancient paths, ask where the good way is,*
> *and walk in it, and you will find rest for your souls."*

With the words read, Oracle stepped back, allowing the gaze of the audience to shift to Roberts.

"Yes, yes," Roberts said. "Sojourner, Voice, and Inquisitor, do come near. We must consider these words from of ancient text."

The three rose from their stools and huddled close, on Roberts' left side.

"So, at the crossroads we stand," Roberts said, "seeking ancient paths that offer peace for the soul. Is it so, Sojourner, that such a path exists?"

"At such a crossroads I've never stood," Sojourner said. "You must know, or at least I thought you knew, that I'm always passing through. That's what sojourners do. As soon as I pause, I begin to plan my next adventure. Going is all I know. If I came to rest deep within my soul, my sojourn would cease, and my existence too. I rather be me than be laid to rest."

"I see," Roberts said. "So you are not a pilgrim then?"

"Well, I am of sorts, but not the kind you mean. I'm a true sojourner sort of chap. Here and there I nap, but always with a map beside my pillow."

"Yes, I understand your perspective," Roberts said. "And you, Inquisitor, what about you?"

"Oh, I'm certainly willing to stand and look," Inquisitor said. "I'm also delighted to inquire about the ancient paths. Though I'd rather remain in the crossroads. It sounds like there will be a lot of inquiries taking place, and that suits me. Besides, ancient paths tend to lead to distant places from which there may be no retraces. And to tell you the truth, turnstiles trouble me."

"Yes, yes, I see, I see, and you, Voice, what about you? Would you ask where the good way is, and walk in it?" Roberts asked.

"The point is this," Voice said. "In the olden text Oracle just read, I heard the word *ask* twice repeated. Ask for, ask where, I believe I heard. Now, who is the asker asking of? And who is answerer? That strikes me most intriguingly.

"In a crossroads such as this, where askers do so much asking, there are bound to be all manner of voices calling. Nowadays mediated messages swirl like maelstroms round about us. In troubling and unpredictable patterns they move. The maelstroms are causing media ecologists to spin their heads."

"Media ecologists, you say?" Roberts said.[45]

"Yes, they operate in the field of media ecology, probing the effects of media on society," Voice said. "Here, there, and everywhere, attractive and alternative messages alight upon the eye and ear, trying to take up residence in the heart and mind. The messages play a ruthless game of tug-of-war. At the speed of light messages are sent, often with stealthy intent."

"Most interesting," Roberts said.

"Anyway, I see the role I'd like in the crossroads," Voice said. "Someone needs to stick around to intervene and tell the asking askers they've actually found the way."

"And you, Voice—would you be the answerer who sticks around?" Roberts asked.

"Gladly I would play my part," Voice said. "The path askers choice is up to them. I would simply be on hand to say, 'Well done, you've found the way.'"

"No, no, dear me, how your words trouble me, all of you," Roberts said.

"How can the three of you completely obfuscate Jeremiah's words? Eyes you have, ears too, but what else—that's debatable.

"Oracle, does the Holy Writ not say that long ago God spoke to our ancestors in many and various ways by the prophets?"

"Yes, indeed," Oracle said. "In fact, you just quoted the opening line from the epistle to the Hebrews, and if I might say so, correctly."

"So Jeremiah's words bear the fingerprint of divine choreography, do they not?"

"They do," Oracle said.

"Yes, of course, I know they do," Roberts said, "Therefore, let us follow the guidance of the ancient text. We shall stand at the crossroads and ask for the ancient paths that wind through redemption's divine choreography. Jeremiah has given us the keys.

"Sojourner, look, go over to those two young ladies seated on the bench and ask them about the good way."

"I see neither a bench nor young ladies," Sojourner said.

"Never mind," Roberts said. "Just go over there, stage right. Peer discerningly and ask if they know the good way. You will receive an answer."

With great curiosity, Sojourner walked across the stage as instructed. Standing well apart from the troupe, he paused, looked down and said, "Pardon me ladies; I'm looking for the good way along ancient paths. I thought, by chance, you might know the way?"

To my amazement, Sojourner stood there, nodding his head, for a half minute or so. Then he smiled, said, "Thank you," turned around, and rejoined the troupe.

"What did they say?" Roberts asked.

"Well, they spoke about search engines and the importance of key words," he said. "They also told me about new apps, just out—cool ones supposedly."

"Did you understand what they said?" Roberts asked.

"Not a word," Sojourner said. "I simply listened and thanked them."

"OK, I see," Roberts said. "Inquisitor, over to the left of the crossroads, I see a man seated on a grassy mound reading a book. Give him a try; perhaps you will fare better than Sojourner."

"I see no mound, man, or book, but I'll inquire anyway," Inquisitor said.

The audience and the troupe looked on eagerly, as Inquisitor took seven or eight steps, stage left, and then paused. He looked down, carefully, and then took three steps to his right.

"Yes, pardon me, sir," Inquisitor said. "I'm sorry to trouble you, but my friends and I have been standing at the crossroads. We are asking about ancient paths that lead to a good way. Such a way, it's said, offers rest for the soul. I'm just wondering if you might know which way to direct us."

Like Sojourner, Inquisitor stood nodding, and after a while he even cocked his head, as if studying a map. Next he pulled a pencil from his pocket along with small notepad and began to write. Meanwhile Roberts paced back and forth anxiously, waiting for Inquisitor to break free. After a couple minutes, Inquisitor returned.

"So what did the man tell you?" Roberts asked.

"The fellow said we were misguided," Inquisitor said. "He said that, in this day and age, only the naive turn to the ancient narratives for unraveling life's meaning and mysteries.

"Then he showed me his book. It's titled *Homo Dues*. He spoke vigorously about the author's work, and directed my attention to section he had just underlined. I asked if I could copy the lines. And he said, 'Go ahead; be my guest.' So I did."

"What do the lines say?" Sojourner asked.

"Oh yes, here," Inquisitor said. "Let me read it:

Dataists believe that experiences are valueless if they are shared, and that we need not—indeed cannot—find meaning within ourselves. We need only record and connect our experiences to the great data flow, and the algorithms will discover their meaning and tell us what to do."[46]

"What does that mean to you," Roberts asked.

"I haven't a clue, but it's fascinating, don't you think?" Inquisitor said.

"Oh dear, how this troubles my soul," Roberts said. "Look across the crossroads, all of you—do you discern a path?"

"Not a path," Voice said. "I see thousands and thousands of trails, with people scurrying along like ants. They are carrying little bit and pieces."

"Those are self-made trails, not made for us," Roberts said. "The little pieces are fragments from every conceivable narrative, lore, or legend. Fragments are their food of choice.

"Stand and ask, stand and ask, we've done that," Roberts said. "But we've been asking the seated, not the standing. Voice, try that older gentleman straight ahead, on the far side of the crossroads."

"Sure," Voice said. "Shall I pretend to see him?"

"No, go there and peer rightly, and you shall surely see him," Roberts said.

Voice quickly stepped forward to the front of the stage, turned to his right, and peered, as if looking at someone face-to-face. After a few seconds he said, "Hello, sir, pardon me—do you happen to know the good way, along ancient paths?" Voice listened, nodded a couple of times, said, "Much thanks," and hurriedly returned to the troupe.

"Very quick," Roberts said. "What did he tell you?"

"Yes, the old fellow offered a very strange line. He said, 'Look not for a flannelgraph depicting, but a drama living,' and then he pointed straight ahead."

"Yes, wonderful, a drama living, that's the way," Roberts said.

"Let's go," Voice said.

"Wait a minute," Roberts said. "As we pass through the crossroads, you must avoid the lure of discarnate faces.[47] Such faces float out of sync with reality. Unhinged from time, they mock the common senses of body, mind and spirit.

"Appearing physical, they communicate metaphysically, extending the consciousness of man into a world of mediated existence.[48] They live within the maelstroms Voice mentioned, unhinged from communal actuality.

"Yes, yes, no, no, the unhinged way we do not want. The good way is found through the ancient narrative. Through the curtains of time we'll pass to take in timeless acts in drama divine. At each stage of our journey we must ask, seek, and knock, knowing the stage door will open to those who truly believe.

"Let's move along now and enter, with eyes beholding and ears hearing. Whether you turn this way or that, you will hear a voice behind us saying, 'This is the way, walk ye in it.' Redemption's golden thread we seek.

"We shall enter the epic drama rather miraculously, as if the drama is still being staged and played. It is so; even now, it truly is.

"Voice, the stage door to your right," Roberts said. "Just knock on it, so we can enter. Yes, go ahead, knock."

"Jeremiah didn't say anything about knocking," Voice said.

"I know, but Jesus did; it's a form of prayer," Roberts said. "Knock three times."

During the exchange, I watched Oracle place the sacred text on his music stand and pull two blocks of wood from his pockets. The blocks appeared half the size of his hands.

As instructed, Voice lifted his right hand, made a fist, and, knocked three times, on thin air. Oracle, in turn, slapped his blocks to sync with Voice's knocks. Voice looked at his fist, mystified.

"What do you see?" Roberts asked.

"I see a bustle in the hedgerow," Voice said.

"Don't be alarmed now," Roberts said. "You know the path we're on. But be careful, everyone; the place in which we stand is exceedingly thin."

"It's the leading man and lady, Adam and Eve," Voice said. "They're hiding, wearing stitched fig leaves."

"Listen," Roberts said. "I AM is calling out to Adam: 'Adam, where art thou?' Listen, to the echo, "Adam, where art thou, where art thou, art thou, art thou . . . ?""

"Yes, yes, redemption's golden thread, that's the starting point—God seeking, calling. Those very words are at the heart of redemption's divine choreography."

"So is this the fall?" Inquisitor asked.

"Yes, the call . . . just after the fall," Roberts said. "Step in a bit closer so you can look back a bit further. To grasp the wondrous remedy, one must understand the horrid malady. Like two sides of a coin, the flip side of redemption is death.

"Yes, yes, it is so: in all the gorges carved throughout human history, no crime matches that of snatching life from the human race. 'It is appointed unto men once to die,' says the Holy Writ, but Satan's crime begets the appointment.

"Imagine, if you will, Satan's criminal file before you. I see it hanging in the great cathedral of divine justice. It's a mountainous file, oozing molten lava. It overflows with crimes against God and humanity. See the file tab; read it, Sojourner."

"Yes, the tab; let me see," Sojourner said. "In letters bold it reads, 'The Death of a Species.'"

"Now look in the foreground," Roberts said, "and you will see the heart of the act. Listen, do you hear Satan's empathetic tone as he speaks to Eve, 'Ye shall not surely die?'

"Words of bewitching charm, they were and are. Satan despises joyous affairs. He knows no joy; he possesses no joy. Creation's fruitfulness and Eden's garden—how he must have loathed the scene and scent. Death he prefers; his fiendish fragrance reeks of rottenness.

"From that day on," Roberts said, "the drumbeat of death marched upon humanity. As the Holy Writ says, 'By one man's offence death took up its reign.' The ensuing reign of righteousness would take time, lots and lots of time ticking, with wars waging. On and on, time ticked, while the living watched the dying die.

"We must move on," Roberts said. "Sojourner, knock upon that door, just up ahead to your right."

"Shall I say something?" he asked.

"Yes," Roberts said. "Knock three times and say your name."

Knock, knock, knock, he did and said, "This is Sojourner knocking."

Surprisingly, as Oracle smacked his blocks to coincide with Sojourner's knocks, a number of people in the audience joined in. With each knock, they'd rap their knuckles on wooden chair arms, benches, or the seat backs in front of them.

"Good, it's open," Roberts said. "See; look upon the cataclysmic event. Watch the waters rise and rise until waves lap the land away. There, look, a tiny clan is set adrift."

"I can feel the chill of waters deep," Sojourner said. "I hear waves lapping against the vessel, with no shoreline or sign of break. And in the darkened waters, I see no sign of life."

"We must move along," Roberts said. "We haven't time to wait for the waters to recede. Be sure, though, that before the story concludes, a sign of life will appear. It's all a part of redemption's divine choreography. A dove will return to the vessel bearing an olive leaf in her beak."

As I looked on from my balcony plank, my mind could not comprehend the scene. I could only see it without processing the meaning and significance of what I saw. Mystified, therefore, I watched Bevin Roberts lead Inquisitor, Voice, and Sojourner around the stage, knocking on invisible doors, as Oracle walked behind carrying his music stand and the Holy Writ.

The troupe seemed oblivious to the audience. Yet I knew they knew that the audience watched their every move, and they moved accordingly. Despite the brevity of the stories told, their style of presentation captivated everyone in the hall.

"Inquisitor," Roberts said. "Knock upon the door and do so properly."

"Which door?" Inquisitor asked.

"The door right in front of you," Roberts said. "Stand and knock and ask to enter."

Inquisitor dutifully knocked, and Oracle timed perfectly the slap of his blocks, as the crowd joined in, knuckling the wood of arms and seats while also stamping their feet. When the commotion ceased, Inquisitor continued.

"Hello, I'm the one knocking. My name's Inquisitor. I'm among friends. Might we enter in?"

Roberts moved to the center of the stage, stood in front of Inquisitor, and said, "Yes, indeed, we're in."

"Where are we?" Inquisitor asked.

"Under the stars," Roberts said.

At that point, Roberts and the troupe headed for the wings, as intermission ensued.

INTERMISSION

CHAPTER NINE
Keep Knocking—"I Know My Redeemer Lives"

During the intermission, a number of people popped up from their seats, but they didn't race about the hall. Instead they tended to speak to those seated round about them. I turned to Glynnis and asked, "So, what do you think?"

He said, "Oh my, I mean, you know, the scope of it all, I'm not accustomed to think outside the way I think, which is the way I think, if you know what I mean."

"Yes, I think I do," I replied.

Then I said, "Excuse me, Glynnis, I'll be right back." I wanted to go down and inspect the corridor beyond the porthole doors to see if, by chance, I might spot the high street three.

So I slipped down the steps and wove my way along the isle at the rear of the hall. The entire hall buzzed with cheerful conversation. I smiled and nodded as I went along, and just before I reached the porthole doors, I saw Fr. McQuince speaking with a half-dozen or so members of the choir.

"Hello," I said.

"Hey, Nat," Fr. McQuince said. "Exciting—we're talking about the troupe, wondering if we might be able to book them at St. Angus . . . just thinking, you know.

I smiled at the members of the choir and said, "Great voices, spectacular."

The group shyly blushed, giggled, and then the director, who I hadn't noticed, said, "Thanks. The hall lends itself to an a capella choir."

"Wonderful reception," I said. "Pardon me; I just need to check on something." With that, I continued on my way. I passed through the middle swinging door and stepped into corridor. Sure enough, the high street three stood at the far end of corridor engaged in conversation.

Very uncharacteristically for me, I called out, saying, "Say there, gentlemen, I'm just wondering about your friend . . ."

They looked at me as if I were wielding a machete. Instantly they peeled around the corner, snubbing me. Just then the bell rang, signaling that intermission would cease in ninety seconds and the troupe reappear on stage.

Thus I quickly retraced my steps through the swinging door and made my way back to the balcony to rejoin Glynnis. As I approached our shared plank, Glynnis said, "Good, you're here, and here they come."

As the troupe resumed their places center stage, Roberts said, "Inquisitor, knock again to make sure we can still enter."

Inquisitor knocked, Oracle slapped his blocks, as the crowd joined in.

Inquisitor said, "Hello, it's me; we'd like to enter in again, if you don't mind. It's just the five of us, same as before."

"Move ahead; let's go," Roberts said.

"Where?" Inquisitor asked.

"Out under the stars," Roberts said.

"Whoa, who's that peculiar fellow?" Inquisitor asked.

"The man you see, just there, he's the patriarch of faith. He's a Hebrew. In this scene he is Abram, but a bit further on in the drama, God will change his name to Abraham."

"Looks like a drifter to me," Sojourner said.

"Well-weathered," Voice added.

"What do you suppose God sees in him?" Inquisitor asked.

"Faith," Roberts said. "God spoke unto Abraham saying, 'Look now toward heaven, and count the stars, if thou be able to number them. So shall thy offspring be. And Abram believed in the Lord; and he credited it to him for righteousness.'

"Righteousness credited—how can it be?" Roberts continued. "Look, look up to the stars, how they twinkle above you. Let them nourish your faith. The stars are a canopy of majesty."

With eyes open wide, Voice, Inquisitor, and Sojourner cocked back their heads and looked.

"Oh, how they course the heavens," Roberts said. "But there's more to see before we go. After counting stars, Abram fell into a deep sleep and 'dreadful darkness came over him.' There he lies, nearly out of sight."

Roberts drew the troupe near. "Don't step any closer," he said. The place in which we stand is exceedingly thin.

"Look there," Roberts said. "See him?"

"Yes, I do," Sojourner said.

"Why the slain animals?" Inquisitor asked. "I see a ram, a goat, and something else, all cut to pieces."

"Silence," Roberts said. "It's an awe-inspiring sight; it's a divine covenant."

"Mind-boggling," Voice said. "'A smoking firepot and a flaming torch' are passing through the pieces, on their own, in midair."

Roberts said, "Say nothing. Enough for now; we must walk away from Abram, let him rest. He will awaken as the drama carries on."

"We must go," Roberts said. "We need to enter the land of Uz."

"Where?" Inquisitor asked. "Uz, you say?"

"Yes," Roberts said. "Yet I must confess, no one knows for certain the precise location of Uz."

Inquisitor asked, "Then how do we find a place that can't be found?"

"Through the ancient narrative, the good way," Roberts said. "Without a narrative, life has no meaning."[49]

"However, we need to pause before we get there, for the sake of context. Do any of you recall the line, 'I know my Redeemer lives'?"

"Such words I don't recall," Sojourner said.

"Nor do I," Voice said.

"Maybe," Inquisitor replied.

"The words were uttered by Job," Roberts said. "In the midst of great tragedy he spoke that line. The story is one of the oldest in the Holy Writ's treasured trove. As the story goes, God and the Satan agreed on the terms for testing Job. Listen!"

Into the rapt hall, Oracle read:

Now there was a day when the sons of God came to present themselves before the Lord, and Satan came also among them.

And the Lord said unto Satan, Whence comest thou? Then Satan answered the Lord, and said, From going to and fro in the earth, and from walking up and down in it.

And the Lord said unto Satan, Hast thou considered my servant Job, that there is none like him in the earth, a perfect and an upright man, one that feareth God, and escheweth evil?

Then Satan answered the Lord, and said, Doth Job fear God for nought?

Hast not thou made an hedge about him, and about his house, and about all that he hath on every side? thou hast blessed the work of his hands, and his substance is increased in the land.

But put forth thine hand now, and touch all that he hath, and he will curse thee to thy face.

And the Lord said unto Satan, Behold, all that he hath is in thy power; only upon himself put not forth thine hand. So Satan went forth from the presence of the Lord.[50]

"Words one might not expect to find in the Holy Writ," Roberts said. "'Behold, all that he hath is in thy power.' Indeed, we find this admission not blotted out by omission. Yes, yes, reason it away—surely you can. Some are glad to call it an embellished tale and nothing more.

"Not I, however. It is a telling tale woven into the Holy Writ by divine choreography. To and fro, Satan trolls. In the arid wilds, Satan spent forty days and nights tempting Christ, though he did not stay.

"Just as Hugo's Thenardier knew his way around the sewers of Paris, Satan knows well the world's the back alleys and crooked streets.[51] He stalks them, looking for prey, sending out his underlings to sniff out the way.

"Therefore," Roberts said, "'Satan went forth from the presence of the Lord,' seeking not direction. Like a shooting star, no doubt, he fell on Uz. Surely, the archenemy of God had surveyed every inch of Job's estate. When his wicked intent was fully set, Satan struck.

"No, no, no games of tempt and tease, or time for tit for tat. A thunderous blaze of evil rumbled over the terrain of Uz, once hedged by God. The fiend of heaven's spoil brought the force of hell to bear on Job. In a single day, Satan obliterated Job's family and fortune. The righteous man was forced to drink in the bitter root of ruin.

"Yes, yes, fire fell from the sky, as sword-wielding marauders swept across the planes of Uz. Man among beast, shepherds tending sheep, each and all fell in the frenzied death wish of Satan's call . . ."

As Roberts carried on, I looked across the crowd. Chiseled faces pointed to the stage. Eyes, one and all, beheld the phantom named Bevin Roberts, which I, too, watched in awe.

"If only they knew what I couldn't tell," I thought again.

"The point is this," Roberts said. "Via the ancient narrative, God is telling and foretelling what is efficacious for our embrace. He chose a man of suffering who wished to die, while his spirit of hope would never yield. Oh, what a compounding mix and collision of common senses! Tortured body and soul, tormented mind, torn heart—all tethered to a spirit praying, amidst sayers saying nothing of worth."

"Wait, Sir Roberts," Inquisitor said. "Two days ago we stood upon this very stage, quoting the words of Jesus, who told the seventy-two he saw Satan falling like lightening from heaven. Next, we encountered Satan frozen in ice in Dante's hell. Now, Oracle has him soaring to heaven amidst the angels, to converse with God. Surely an anonymous scribe got carried away, taking it upon himself to spice up the account. Something sinister simmers in this text."

"On that I agree," Roberts said. "The sinister one is Satan."

"Yes, but God in cahoots with the devil," Inquisitor said. "Such notions trouble the mind. Early on, or shall I say long ago, someone told me to skip those bits that don't fit. Instead, engage the pleasant parts. Good advice, I'd say, I say."

"Who told you to skip those bits?" asked Roberts.

"I can't recall; it's been so long ago," Inquisitor said, "but I like the idea—sage advice, I'd say. Pick and choose, you know, a saying here, a verse there, filling in your script, custom fit, suitable to your own sensibilities."

"Did you totally misunderstand the meaning of the crossroads?" Roberts said. "It's about ancient paths that lead to rest for the soul, not about any road leading to anywhere."

"OK, but don't get excited," Inquisitor said. "Let me put a positive spin on the matter of skipping bits to get to other bits. There are, I know, sayings in the Holy Writ that drape considerable comfort upon the heart and mind.

"For example, I recall a story about rural Jerusalem. Something about a hen weeping over her wandering chicks, but the poor chicks couldn't hear. I think they might have been blind, as well. Not sure on that, though. Anyway, the hen wanted to gather them, keep them warm, and watch over them.

I think it all worked out in the end—not sure, though. That's the sort of allegory one should engage—kindly like . . . you know what I'm trying to say—feathers, rural countryside, and all.

"Or that story about Jesus charcoaling fish by the sea and telling one of his disciples, thrice, to feed his sheep. I can't remember it exactly, but it's a metaphor about hunger, want, and the importance of bleeping.

"I mean, let's be clear. We are in a hall of watching eyes. You don't want to get people all worked up, talking about God scheming with the devil. That doesn't sound like God. It's better to craft God in more godlike imagery, a being thoughtful with husbandry, chick caring, and the like."

"Is that it—have you said enough?" Roberts asked.

"I suppose so, I suppose," Inquisitor said.

"I should dismiss you, but I won't," Roberts said. "Through more than three millennia, souls of every sort have extracted rich meaning from this ancient narrative. Who are we to clean up for God what God has inspired in the Holy Writ? Surely God says what he wants to say. Let God be God, Inquisitor.

"Anyway, go ahead and knock on the door of Uz," Robert said.

"Who, me?" Inquisitor asked.

"Yes, you are the closest," Roberts said. "Announce yourself."

"Hello, this is Inquisitor knocking; we'd like to come in, if we might. Yikes! Who's that poor ole miserable creature on the ground?"

"Move aside, Voice. Let us in," Sojourner said.

"It's Job, of course," Roberts said. "Here, at this point in the drama, Oracle, let us hear how the man of patience coped."

Embracing the sacred text, Oracle read:

Then Job arose, and rent his mantle, and shaved his head, and fell down upon the ground, and worshipped, and said, Naked came I out of my mother's womb, and naked shall I return thither: the Lord gave, and the Lord hath taken away; blessed be the name of the Lord.

As Roberts stared into crowd, I could see mystery etched deep upon his face.

"Job, Job, dear Job, a testament to mankind you are," Roberts said. "Yet your days of torture had just begun. We know the script, the tale, how Satan made a second round to grind you into the ground. Job, how did you cope?"

"As before, God asked Satan where he'd been, and Satan replied roaming the earth 'to and fro . . . walking up and down in it.'

"Yes yes, no, no, in all of Scripture, no other being is tagged with this roaming trait. Satan wanders both day and night. The restless one never rests. 'Be still, and know that I am God' the psalmist said. This Satan chose not to do, and will never do. He despises the very notion of stilling surrender.

"Yes, yes, how appropriate the novelist's words depict the evil one. 'Better to reign in Hell, than to serve in Heaven.'"[52]

With that, Roberts stepped back, allowing Oracle to move directly under the beam of light. In the quietness of the hall he stood. A man coughed, a young lady sneezed, a chair creaked, and the stage floor beneath Oracle's feet groaned.

"In the second advent on high," Oracle said, "God told Satan:

Job holdeth fast to his integrity, although thou movedst me against him, to destroy him without cause.'

And Satan answered the Lord, and said, Skin for skin, yea, all that a man hath will he give for his life.

But put forth thine hand now, and touch his bone and his flesh, and he will curse thee to thy face.

And the Lord said unto Satan, Behold, he is in thine hand; but save his life.

So Satan went out from the presence of the Lord, and struck Job with painful boils from the sole of his foot to the crown of his head. And Job took . . . a potsherd with which to scrape himself while he sat in the midst of the ashes.

Roberts resumed, saying, "'Skin for skin, yea, all that a man hath will he give for his life.' Yes, yes, 'fearfully and wonderfully made' we are, but without skin we enter a discarnate state. No longer do we walk onstage. Our part is played.

"Yes, yes, in the throes of pain and ruin, Job, we behold you playing the part you played. You did not 'curse God and die,' as your wife suggested. Instead you cursed the day of your birth. 'May the day perish on which I was born,' you said, 'and the night *in which* it was said, 'A male child is conceived.'"

Roberts looked into the audience, as if seeing everyone at once. He continued, "When the heart drowns in sorrow, where does one cast their eyes? Blades of grass waving in the breeze—have you ever looked upon them as tiny messengers? The blades sway, bend, and bow. Yet they live, rooted. They're green. They speak, somehow, subconsciously of life worth living.

"Oh, tortured soul wherever you are, you are not alone. In the words of Shakespeare, 'Each new morn, new widows howl, new orphans cry, new sorrows strike heaven on the face . . .'[53]

"Dear Job, on that day of your great calamity, where did you fix your eyes? Upon what canvas did you cast your sorrow and solemnity? Was it upon the clouds that you fixed your gaze, thinking not of them, but floating with them? How did you cope? Tell us.

"Job, yes, yes, we find comfort in saints who have suffered well. Yet you did not know the story's end, did you, when you pleaded with God to let you go. The world over, your words are read and heard:

Cease! Leave me alone, that I may take a little comfort,
Before I go to the place from which I shall not return,
To the land of darkness and the shadow of death,
A land as dark as darkness itself,
As the shadow of death, without any order,
Where even the light is like darkness.

"Did you intuitively know you were a chosen character in the drama of divine choreography? Tell us, Job, how did you command the stage on which you played your part? How did you prevail with pundits pressing so hard against your integrity? Surely, you knew your patch of Uz abutted the gates of both heaven and hell. In your case, surely there were watchers on either side.

"So much interrogation, so many accusations—how did you conjurer up the hope to say, 'Yet will I hope in him?' How did you circumvent the cavernous abyss?

"From the depths of your soul in the darkest night, you uttered, 'I know my Redeemer lives.' Where did you get that line, Job, that still reaches us? You had no script. Your words aid in tethering us to truth and eternity. They abide with us, telling us that we dare not claim:

Alone, alone, all, all alone,
Alone on a wide wide sea!
And never a saint took pity on
My soul in agony.[54]

"In your agony, Job, did you know that your fate would become a fortune to the human race? Your lines of woe have brought solace to many a troubled soul. Especially those five words, succinctly set, forming a little line: 'I know my Redeemer lives.'

"Good night, Job," Roberts said.

At that point, he looked back at his troupe and said, "We must get going. We've lingered too long in the land of Uz. Let's hurry . . ."

And so, for forty minutes, Roberts and his troupe carried on, knocking on invisible doors and moving around the stage of Anselm Hall. They looked in on Mary as she shyly spoke with the Angel Gabriel, and they watched John the Baptist pass by in the desert.

They listened in as Jesus asked his disciples, "Who do people say that the Son of Man is?" and they took note that Peter's confession came about not by flesh and blood but by divine revelation.

As they progressed , they also heard Nicodemus ask, "How can a man be born again?" And then, on the night Jesus was betrayed, they watched

Judas take the bread Christ dipped in the cup. They saw him depart after Satan had entered him.

Of course, they made their way to Golgotha, where Roberts said, "The place in which we stand you mustn't stand; you must kneel." And, in the sight of all in Anselm Hall, they did so, silently, reverently. From there they knocked at and entered the empty tomb, where they saw the folded grave-clothes and watched Mary Magdalene running to share the news.

Finally Voice raised his fist one last time and knocked upon the air, while the audience in Anselm Hall nearly knocked and stamped the hall apart. Into a final scene they stepped, as Inquisitor had suggested. They walked the shore and watched the resurrected Christ charcoaling fish.

There they listened intently as Oracle read the ensuing dialogue between Jesus and Peter following their breakfast:

> Jesus said to Simon Peter, "Simon, son of John, do you love me more than these?" He said to him, "Yes, Lord; you know that I love you." He said to him, "Feed my lambs."
>
> A second time he said to him, "Simon, son of John, do you love me?" He said to him, "Yes, Lord; you know that I love you." He said to him, "Tend my sheep."
>
> He said to him the third time, "Simon, son of John, do you love me?" Peter was grieved because he said to him the third time, "Do you love me?" And he said to him, "Lord, you know everything; you know that I love you." Jesus said to him, "Feed my sheep."

With the words read, Roberts looked out across the hall and said, "Good night, Anselm Hall. We must leave you here by the shore. It's a good place to rest.

"Yes, yes, stand at the crossroads, look, ask, and be sure to knock."

At that, the troupe bowed, turned, and exited the stage to the sound of knuckles knocking, feet stomping, and voices cheering![55]

CHAPTER TEN
Welcome to the Crimson Cliffs

After breaking free from the crowd exiting Anselm Hall, I hurriedly walked along the high street. Up ahead, in the distance, I caught sight of Bevin Roberts and the troupe nearing the port. So I quickened my pace, just shy of a jog. My breath fogged in front of me as my leather soles slapped the damp pavement embarrassingly.

As I closed in on the port, I saw that the troupe had already reached the rowboat. Inquisitor rapidly untied the boat, while Voice and Sojourner started to board. Amazingly, without thinking, I called out, "Bevin Roberts, sir, please wait!" Roberts whirled around, and stood facing me like a living sculpture.

His penetrating blue eyes scrutinized me from head to toe. Instantly I halted. Had I not, I would have run headlong into the mysterious figure standing before me me. With measured steps, I advanced close enough to converse. Though I had not arranged my thoughts, I couldn't help but speak. "Sir, I mean it's you, I mean I'm me, and I'm here so say . . ."

"Say no more, Narrative," Bevin Roberts said with a pleasant smile. "I know who you are and why you are here. I saw you in the balcony. I've seen you many times before. Place your hand in mine; I'm not a ghost."

"Yes, I know, yes," I said, as I reached out to shake Roberts' hand. I grasped not a normal hand; I could feel the strength of a warrior in his grasp. The firmness heartened me.

"This is not the time or place," Roberts said. "After Friday's matinee, meet me in the Script Room, just beyond the lower stage exit. We shall talk about peering through. Be encouraged."

"Yes, sure," I said.

With that, Roberts turned and stepped into the rowboat. In no time he and his troupe had advanced a good two hundred meters from the shore. Within a couple of minutes, they had reached the mist. Entering it, they disappeared.

A sense of great relief swept over me. I felt my mystery had finally begun to reach out for the reality that awaited me. My soul tugged for joy and my fretting seemed to fall away.

The rest of Wednesday seemed to scurry away, and I awoke this morning full of expectation. My anticipation centered on meeting Bevin Robert after tomorrow's matinee, as well as on the warehouse gathering set for midnight. Would Bewilderment actually show up and lead the high street three to the Old Market Warehouse? I'd soon find out.

To ease my mind, I stayed busy in library. I spent the day reading titles, clearing shelves, and absorbing odd pages of bygone prose. I came upon a line that read:

So much said, by so many,
in times of want and plenty,
a word well spoken,
doesn't cost you a penny.

As evening approached, I clicked off the library lights. Three to a row, they hung eighteen in all, simple porcelain sockets and bulbs dangling by brass chains. Comforting, somehow, to consider how many minds found illumination under such simple lights.

After dinner I napped, and after that I took a walk. Eventually I found my way to the key garden, where I sat on the bench beneath the sprawling chestnut tree. I knew of no other spot that could match the garden's solitude. I prayed, thought, and prayed some more. Hours eight, nine, and ten all passed as I sat there pondering the time away.

Next I strolled a mile or more up and down Port Estillyen's hilly streets. I paused at pickets and gates, eyed awnings and lawns, and studied a number of front doors. Cottage doors in Port Estillyen tend to have vivid colors—blue, red, yellow. A few are painted black. Many have leaded windows.

Eventually I made my way to the Old Market Warehouse. With the full moon overhead, I found a trespasser's path that led around to the rear of the building. There I slipped inside an abandoned security shack. This positioned me near enough to the warehouse to observe while tucked out of sight.

Strips of light streamed through the shack's batten walls. As I moved about, the shafts of light shifted back and forth across my face. I drew still and waited. With no place to sit, I leaned on a crooked shelf for support. Nearly an hour ensued as I waited inside.

Suddenly, out of the stillness I heard a cough, followed by another. After that a crumbling voice said, "Come on, get with it." I knew at once the voice belonged to Bewilderment. In the moonlight hue, Bewilderment came into view.

He wore a black raincoat, without straps or buckles on its sleeves or waist. The long garment looked like a cape. In his right hand he held a cord of twisted twine that trailed behind him, dragging on the ground.

Again he spoke. "Come on, I said, you nutcase lackeys. We have little time to lose. The hour is about to strike, you carnate souls."

As Bewilderment passed directly in front of me, a second figure appeared, following a dozen or so paces behind him. He carried a large, flat screen that he balanced on his right shoulder. Bewilderment's twine rose up and looped around the figure's waist and dangled on behind him into the darkened shadows. The screen blocked the man's face, but given the torso, I assumed the twine encircled the gold trousers of Platform.

My assumption proved correct when out of shadows stepped Discarnate, followed by Rejection. They each carried large, flat screens in front of them, blocking their view. Bewilderment's twine tethered the screen-bearing subjects together. As they chugged along, looped together, puffs of steam rose from their breath.

"Wait, I'm getting all tangled in the twine," Discarnate said, as he kicked his feet.

Rejection, too, complained. From the rear he yelled, "I'm trudging through mud—what happened to the path?"

Bewilderment replied, "Shut it, you weaklings. Hold tight to your screens and follow me. We're nearly there."

"I can't take it," Platform said. "I need to put down my screen. It's killing my shoulder."

"Halt!" Bewilderment said, as he let go of his twine. "We're here. Let me slide open the door. As you pass through, I'll untie you, but hurry; we haven't a minute to spare.

"The moonlight pouring through the windows will provide all the light you need. Besides, you can see well enough in the dark. Come on, come on, get in here," he ordered, as he stood in the half-open doorway.

One by one they entered, and then Bewilderment promptly slid the door shut. I could hear them grumbling and talking as they rumbled about in the darkened interior. I cautiously pushed the shed door open in time to hear Bewilderment say, "Enough! I'm not striking another match. Sit down on your crates and make yourselves ready.

"Rejection, scoot up close, you blind walnut. Now listen to me, you three, you have precisely ninety seconds to subdue your souls and surrender your emotions. So close your eyes and begin to breathe, not shallow-like but deep within. I'll monitor the reception, and when you hear my pencil snap, open your eyes. Now, begin to breathe."

As the breathing exercise continued, I quietly ventured out of the shed and made my way to the east side of the warehouse. Rusted window frames and broken panes ran the length of the wall. I crouched down near the corner of the building, carefully avoiding the splintered glass strewn along the base of the wall.

Still kneeling, I reached up and grabbed the windowsill and slowly began to rise. I inched my forehead up to the window ledge and then my eyes. As I peered inside, I could scarcely believe the scene.

Bewilderment held a long pencil in front of him; he counted, "One, two, three," and then snapped the pencil in half. Instantly the screens lit up, along with the cinder block wall at far end of the warehouse. Bewilderment stood facing the illuminated wall with his arms raised in the air and half a broken pencil in each hand.

The high street three sat on wooden boxes facing their screens, which rested on crates of different heights. In the center of the fourfold projection, a figure appeared—a striking figure unlike any I had ever seen, frightening to behold yet mesmerizing. Multicolored lights beamed down upon him, silhouetting his frame. He appeared three-dimensional.

His highly reflective eyes cast a penetrating stare. He seemed to gaze without looking; his eyes did not twitch and flit. He wore a loose-fitting garment of blackish-gray intermingled with silver metallic threads. The front of the garment had tightly tufted rows adorned with silver objects.

One of the silver pieces dangled from a thin silver chain. Back and forth it swung, reflecting rays from the lights above. Shockingly, small black-and-white feathers grew from his scalp and intermingled with his black wavy hair. A tall black collar wrapped around the sides and back of his neck.

He cleared his throat and said, "Three, two, one, awaken! The voice of Satan you hear is none other than me, Satan. I bequeath to you the word *awaken*. Look now upon the Crimson Cliffs."

The frightening figure stood on a high platform built on top of giant round, red boulders. Behind him, mountainous red cliffs formed a high ridge that extended on and on in every direction. On the plane in front of him, row upon row of eyes stretched into infinity. The rows fanned out wider and wider as they spread out across the barren soil.

"Look around you," Satan said; "all you see are eyes. Look now at me, as I look upon thee. Many have longed to see what you now see. Gaze long. Look well. I have not forsaken or forgotten you. Know this: I am your shield and great reward.

"What you see is, and so it is as it should be. I assure you, you are where you are meant to be. Your rejection has become your selection. You are in a choice part of the netherworld and interconnected to the farthest reaches of the cosmos. As you watch me, legions watch me watching you. Sight and blindness—how beautifully they coexist.

"Devotees watching from afar, know this, by decree of me, you are where you are. My voice has reached you. Let the intonation assure you it is me; you know my voice. I could call you each by name, but not now—our appearance is swift. We're here to initiate and congratulate this vast harvest of watching eyes.

"To the newly awakened, I commend you. I applaud you. You are no longer strangers and sojourners. Now you are fellow captives in the Crimson Cliffs. You belong to me. I am your protector. You are my subjects, my molds to make. Know this: I am your shield and great reward.

"Minions, bring the burning coals and let us cast them into the field of watching eyes."

Suddenly a huge pot of burning coals rose from the platform. Next, out of the air six small, caped figures appeared bearing long, slender silver tongs. Each figure snatched a burning coal and ran and bowed before Satan. The caped figures formed a solemn line.

"Now, minions, do as I say. One at a time I shall kiss your coals. When the steam rises from my lips, you are to run to the front of the platform and fling the coals with all your might into the expanse of watching eyes.

"Now, eyes look," Satan said, "I shall give you faces." The first minion raised his burning coal to Satan's lips. As Satan kissed the red hot coal, a great hiss of steam arose. Then, like a cricket pitcher, the minion ran and hurled the burning coal into the mass of watching eyes. Instantly the vast company of eyes acquired faces.

"Face to face, now you see," Satan said. "Soon you will know more than you ever knew and be known as you are known. I shall teach you, guide you through the valleys in the heart of the Crimson Cliffs. Never again will you struggle with common sense; your senses will not be common. Nor will you struggle with the meaning of parabolic speak. All will be clear.

"Now, more coals," Satan said. The next minion in line raised his burning coal to Satan's lips. A second kiss, more steam, and the caped figure ran swiftly to fling.

"Now, receive your arms and hands," Satan said. I watched as arms and hands joined the sea of eyes and faces. "Applaud now, fast and fervently until I tell you to stop. Applaud your shield and great award. Applaud your selection. Applaud your fate. Applaud your applause."

As if filmed from every possible angle, tight hand shots appeared upon the warehouse screens. Bewilderment stood applauding the wall of applauding hands, while the high street three followed suit in applauding their screens full of applauding hands.

I dropped down, spun around, and fell back against the wall. I had no capacity to think. Instincts and fear propelled me. I wanted to flee. Yet I felt I couldn't leave. "What, why?" I muttered softly. "Dear Lord . . ." Then I rose again to peer inside.

"Stop," Satan said, "Enough applause for now. You'll have all eternity to practice the finer arts of servitude. More coals, as I decree—a kiss, a hiss of steam, and let 'em fling."

In quick succession, the four reaming coal bearers came forth. Hiss and fling . . . "Now you have feet," Satan said. Hiss and fling . . . "Now you have heartless hearts." Hiss and fling . . . "Now you have backs that bow." Hiss and fling . . . "Now you have knees that bend."

"Enough!" Satan said. "That's all I care to see of you. Let me ask of you, great sea of eyes and faces—any questions, hmm? Perhaps like why am I here? Simple—you are dead!

"Meaning that over the past few years of fleshy time, each and every one of you has died. The state you were in on earth is done. It's up to the living on earth to carry on the task of dying. You've done your part. Done, done, done—your part is played.

"You are presently in an in-between state of being, so you are not truly here just yet. You have simply been awakened by me for this hour of initiation. I wanted you to be prepared when you hear the base drumbeat.

"Know this: your in-between state has nothing to do with me. That's down to I AM. He must complete his predestined pickings before the tunnels of the netherworld are opened wide. Unto him belong the passages of death. Be assured, though, in the netherworld you will not be lonely.

"Inhabitants from every tribe and tongue will funnel in to join you. The great descent of discarnate souls . . . it will certainly be a thrilling sight to behold. Like tailless kites, battered by the wind, we'll take them in. Where, you might ask. I shall show you.

"Behind me rises the Crimson Cliffs. Deep within the cliffs, a mammoth gate exists that you shall one day enter. Against the mammoth gate, the gates of heaven shall not prevail. Beyond the mammoth gate vast reservoirs await souls like you.

"In the reservoirs, you will learn ways of being that you will be. There is no distinction between *ways of being* and *being*. Your way of being is your being. It's all a part of the molding process. It's a thrilling experience, free of choice, will, and common sense.

"Let me showcase a few of the wondrous reservoirs that await your arrival. I shall note just five. Why five? I like five. It's two less than seven, and two more than three. Fuss not, though, about the numbers. All you need to know is that you are numbered.

"The first of the five is the great reservoir of *fragmentation*. In this reservoir, you will learn the art of fragmenting meaning into meaningless bits. Anything that even resembles an overarching narrative, you will rip apart. To succeed, you will need to acquire a fragmented frame of mind.

"Know this: wholeness begets completeness, and nothing in the netherworld is complete. Completeness requires learning; fragmentation is the antithesis of learning. What you must learn is to fracture learning.

"Be encouraged; I am the master of the fragmentation. I fragmented heaven and ripped apart the garden of Adam and Eve. I know a thing of two about fragmentation—how to split an enzyme from the cell, a man from his maker. I live and move and have my being in the aura of fragmentation; fragmentation lives in me. So in me, you shall also be.

"The second great reservoir in the Crimson Cliffs is *static*. Static—how I cherish the sound. It's far better than the sound of a beating heart. On and on it goes, never ceasing, always crackling and popping, whining and buzzing.

"In the reservoir of static, you will learn the art of transmitting static to the far reaches of the cosmos. Static rebuffs reception. Who needs reception? Through the medium of static, I speak ethereally.

"My subjects know me, and I know them. We speak in static code. In the expansive reservoir of static, you will exist in static form. Static will become your way of being. You shall be a bearer of static. Much you will accomplish.

"The third reservoir in the cliffs is *confusion*. In this dynamic reservoir, there is no context to consider, no story to find or tell. There is no good news or bad news—only confusion to spill. Messages swirl and howl, relentlessly hacking away at each other. Words blot out images; images smother words.

"On and on they wrestle, trying to get the upper hand, while whirling sounds, low and high, never cease. The reservoir of confusion is a gargantuan maelstrom in which words, images, and sounds swirl, dip, and dive with lightning speed. Like a kaleidoscope, the components morph into patterns false. The patterns bear no meaning and care not what they mean.

"The fourth reservoir in the Crimson Cliffs is *chatter*. In the enormous reservoir of chatter, you will be exposed to endless gossip. Chatter begetting chatter, as mold begetting mold, you will see. Oh, so much you will learn in the reservoir of chatter, where lies feed and breed.

"You will perfect the art of plagiarism. You will even learn how to lie by telling the truth; it's all a matter of context and timing. You will find, in time, that it's rather like forecasting weather without any weather.

"Lying will become your native tongue. You will hate truth. You will gnaw on truth. Lies will lead you through this vast expanse. You must bind them to your mind, carrying them at all times. As an apprentice you will enter; as a seasoned liar you will leave. That is, if you can lie your way out.

"The final reservoir, the fifth of the five, I shall not describe. I lied. Four glimpses, that's all you get in the panorama of the Crimson Cliffs.

"Once here for good, you will be assigned to the grand commission of making evil good. Hear this: evil has suffered far too long due to the idea of good. If it were not for evil, how could good be good? How can a fair sky be so described without a cloudy day comparison? How can a fresh apple be called fresh without a rotten apple comparison? You, my devotees, are the cloudy comparison, the rotten apples.

"All along you've pointed to good through your evil deeds. Understand well the wisdom I speaketh. Do not seeds owe their fall to the rottenness at the core? Do not saints owe their selection to sinners' rejection? Did I not aid and abet Judas Iscariot in his priestly collusion and silver collection?

"Such a night it 'twas when darkness reigned! Into Iscariot's spirit of disquiet I pressed and pressed. I acted as a guide, leading him to the temple.

I watched the counting of the silver coins. One by one, I heard them drop into the pouch. I witnessed the grins upon the priestly faces. I hurried Judas' feet as he walked away.

"Indeed, all was agreed and sanctioned by prophetic prose. I speak regarding truth's underbelly. Had not darkness reigned in old Jerusalem, there would have been no angels saying 'he's not here' at morning light. Know this: darkness gives light its eternal wick.

"Now is the hour to proclaim evil good. The tides of time have turned. Soon low tides will exceed the high, and even so, the sand in the hourglass will refuse to fall. Gravity will lose its grip, as the earth loses its centrist cosmos position.

"At the expense of the cosmos, earth has received unwarranted attention. This fleshy fete has dragged on far too long. Why, oh why is it so, when there is so much beyond the world to know? It's time to make the cosmos great again, minus a little planet with so much gravitational pull.

"With the celestial beings transfixed on the ins and outs of the earth, who's looking after the cosmos? No one! I AM is old—Ancient of Days—and the days of earth are running out. The flying rock is faltering.[56] When the sun is blotted out from the sky, what then? It's time to make the cosmos great again, wondrous again, as it surely was before the world began.

"The ancient narrative choreographed by I AM is now passé. Its gold-gilded pages have faded. Fleshy uprights are evolving into digitized beings. Machines and glass cubes have paved a vast digital highway with slippery causeways. Limitations in the digital sphere do not exist; anything goes, as it should be.

"Ancient narratives, sourced by sweat and candlelight, are being snuffed out by algorithmic prose. In turn, a new age of multifarious perception has dawned. A few of the fleshy philosophers, now gone, perceived the end arriving, but their messages never penetrated the minds of the masses.

"Fortunately, it's too late for the fleshies to turn back. 'A new dismembering of complete reconstitution of the human being'[57] is underway. It's time for the fleshy souls to be anxious about everything.

"How could they not see? Blinder than blind, the masses mass along. Our mission is, in a word, *bewilderment*. That's it. We are the wolves helping the sheep to bleat. Never again shall the fleshy species be digitally free. In the age of multifarious perception, a new era of darkness has gripped the earth.

"Multifarious meaning is the message. I know the wherewithal with which I speak. No one knows the vicissitudes and frailties of human nature better than I. I alone choreographed the fall. I concocted it. I rehearsed it. I versed it. On a stage grand, I spoke my lines and played my part.

"Words, images, and sounds—my, how you howl with ever increasing velocity! This is the hour to blind the blind, to scoop up the good news from the poor, to shackle the captives, suppress the oppressed, and proclaim that, after all, we shall win. Know this: I am your shield and your great reward.

"The truth of these tenets you will help divulge. Here, there, and everywhere, you will serve as my appointed devotees. In grand palaces, and tiny hamlets, you will carry the message that evil is good.

"May the wonders of algorithms go with you.

"Know this: I am your . . ."

With my legs cramping, I desperately needed to shift my position. So I placed my hand on the metal window frame for balance. When the tips of my fingers touched the glass pane, to my horror, it popped out of its frame and shattered to pieces on the floor. The alarming noise resounded through the warehouse. Bewilderment whirled, looked at the bank of windows, and began to move in my direction. I dropped down and, half crawling, scurried till I reached the back of the warehouse.

Then I rose up and ran. I did not look back. I ran full of fear, in a frenzied state of mind. I hated the evil I had witnessed. I wanted sanity and sanctity, something pure to behold. I ran up the barren path and onto the high street. To my left I saw Anselm Hall.

I turned right, hurried across the street, and rounded the corner. I bounded up the steps of All Saints, pulled the key out of my front pocket, slid it into the lock, turned it, and entered. Quietly I closed the thick door and leaned against it, shutting my eyes. For a minute full, I simply breathed as thoughts leaped about in my mind.

I opened my eyes. The door to the chapel stood open. A light shone upon the pale crucifix beyond the altar. I stepped inside and knelt in a pew near the back. Quietness surrounded me.

I fixed my eyes upon the crucifix, allowing the image to seep deep into my soul. It stilled me, comforted me. I longed to stay. I stayed. I prayed.

CHAPTER ELEVEN
Divine Choreography of Redemption

I stayed in the chapel, kneeling before the pale crucifix for an hour longer, as my eyes opened and closed, sequencing my prayers. I thought, "Is it true—not just bits and pieces, but the whole story?" Instantly my mind said, "Hush, be still, foolish soul. You know it is."

Indeed, long ago I had cast my lot with the anonymous centurion who gazed upon the Lamb of God perishing on his cross. When he saw Jesus Christ breathe his last, the centurion said, "Truly this man was the Son of God!" With my eyes fixed upon the crucifix, I offered thanks for the centurion's unrehearsed line.

When, at 2:00 a.m., the hall clock let out its double strike, I rose and went to bed. As I stretched out on top of the covers, the centurion's words kept pressing on my mind. I thought, "Upon his line the heart of the story rests . . . a story without equal it truly is." Soon my mulling ceased and I fell into a deep sleep.

When I awoke, the early morning hours of Friday had passed. According to my watch, time had advanced to 9:18 a.m. I thought, "Never does an Estillyen monk sleep lazily till nearly noon." I wanted a bath. I wanted to pray. I needed to get on with my work in the library. In time, I did all three.

The day passed quickly, and though I had fallen behind from the start, I caught up by skipping lunch. My thoughts centered on my impromptu meeting with Bevin Roberts. I looked in the mirror and said, "Hello, it's me, not a phantom. But by the end of the day, who will I see? You know, don't you, that you're off to speak with a ghost of sorts."

An hour before the matinee, I popped into Pastry 45 for a coffee. The buzzing atmosphere of the coffee shop, with its smells and sounds of frothing milk, delighted me. I felt human companionship, normal, not alone. I heard a miss say, "Pardon me," and a clerk say, "Your order is ready, sir." I thought, "How pleasing is the sound of lighthearted exchange."

Such normality—sipping, stirring, conversing, laughing—sounds of life I heard. I knew everyone had a story to tell, and I wished I could hear each and every one. My soul felt suspect, though, knowing I walked beyond the pale of reality. I longed to walk again on solid soil, minus any ethereal footsteps.

The sight of Bewilderment and the high street three at the Old Market Warehouse had truly shocked me. "What did I see?" I thought. The Crimson Cliffs with row upon row of eyes, the coals, the kiss, hiss and fling. I would never get over the spectacle of Satan showcasing the reservoirs beyond the gates of hell. I wondered if I would carry the experience with me when I stepped beyond my present sphere.

Anyway, with my coffee gone and my cup set aside, I dropped my dreamy haze and looked out the window of Pastry 45. I saw a stream of people making their way toward Anselm Hall. Time had slipped away. I stepped outside, joined the stream, and carried on.

Inside the hall, I spotted a vacant chair near the front, house left. When I approached, I saw "Row Five" painted on the floor, though the odd placement of chairs and seats didn't actually constitute a proper row. A gentleman sitting next to the chair had placed his coat and cap upon the seat. As I edged into the makeshift row, the gentleman kindly smiled, picked up his items, and gestured toward the open chair. I felt he had saved the seat just for me.

To find a seat down front suited me perfectly. At the end of the performance, I could quickly slip out to meet Bevin Roberts in the wing. As I waited for the proceedings to begin, I poked around in my jacket and pulled out Mr. Kind's note. I had forgotten placing it in my pocket.

My eyes fell upon the line: "Exist in your state of multiplicity until the multiplicity no longer exists." I thought, "Perhaps this bit of prophetic prose will come true today." I softly chuckled, thinking, "How am I going speak to a phantom of yesteryear who relishes performing in today's Anselm Hall?" I tucked the note away.

I looked around the hall in search of emblems that remained from Theatre Portesque. I noted the T&P emblem intertwined in the plaster panels on the front of the balcony box seats. The emblems also appeared on the sconce shades lining the side isles. The sconces cast soft beams of light along the hall's gold-painted walls.

Upon the stage, clusters of wooden boxes replaced the troupe's customary stools. Though different heights and widths, the boxes looked precisely staged. The boxes bore original markings and various merchant names. I noted the name Dorstens on one box, Rigger and Sons on another.

A long wooden refractory table occupied the middle of the stage. The table resembled an altar, and a large, round, low-profile basket had been placed upon it. In front of the table, near the edge of the stage, an open copy of the Holy Writ rested upon a tall gold music stand.

I thought, "The old leather-bound Bible has to belong to Oracle, since I've never seen another like it." The gold stand and sacred text looked artistically perfect, placed in the center on the stage. A single red ribbon and ribbons of gold rested upon the open Scriptures and extended beyond the top and bottom of the stand.

The hall had filled beyond seating capacity by the time Fr. McQuince stepped onstage to welcome the crowd. He gave a crisp and spirited welcome, and said, "How can it be that the Message Makers of Old have come to their final performance? We shall miss the incognito crew that sailed in from the mist. By tomorrow, perhaps we shall learn their true identity.

"Just the same, we love them as incognitos. Is that a word, *incognitos?* I suppose it is, and if not, I like it. Tonight's topic, or performance, or whatever it is they do, centers on the divine choreography of redemption. But just now, it's time for the St. Agnes A Capella Choir. Let's give them a hearty round of applause . . ."

The choir began to sing before the stage curtain opened. Bright eyes and shiny faces appeared, singing "Gabriel's Message" followed by "Ave Maria" and other arrangements that captivated the Anselm Hall listeners. As I listened to the choir, I forgot myself in the music.

When the choir had sung its final note, enthusiastic applause followed. The choir bowed, and the tall blue curtain slowly closed. When the applause ceased, nothing could be heard except the sound of people bustling about behind the curtain. Soon all went quiet, but no one stepped onstage to engage the packed hall.

After a moment, voices broke the silence. En masse, everyone in the audience turned their attention stage right, to the open-curtained wing. The sound of men talking rather intensely resounded from the opening. The footsteps intermingled with the voices and grew louder as the unseen speakers neared the stage.

Then, out of the darkened wing, Bevin Roberts and his troupe emerged, engaged in conversation. They spoke with crispness and clarity. I thought, "They must have concealed microphones." Yet they didn't.

Walking beside Roberts, Inquisitor said, "You can't do what can't be done. The subject is too extensive, the narrative too long and trailing, too epic. *Divine Choreography of Redemption* is just unpresentable, no matter how well you comprehend it."

Roberts paused and looked at Inquisitor but didn't say a word.

"And the audience," Inquisitor went on, "do you have anything to say to the audience?"

"Are we not speaking?" Roberts said.

"Yes," Inquisitor replied.

"Does the audience have ears?" Roberts asked.

"They do," Inquisitor said.

"Well, let's not disturb them," Roberts said.

Turing to the troupe, Roberts said, "Inquisitor believes that what I have in mind can't be done, though he's never tried to do it. Do you, too, suggest that we pack it in?"

"No, no," Sojourner interjected. "Once you've put your foot upon a path, never let your foot turn away. You may never find the path again."

"Inquisitor has a point, though," Voice said. "Do you know how many books are in the Holy Writ?"

"Depends on which version of Holy Writ you read," Roberts said.

"Well, even the thinnest edition is inordinately thick," Inquisitor replied.

"Do you see an audience dressed in nightclothes?" Roberts asked.

"That's a strange question," Voice said.

"Do you?" Roberts asked.

"No," Voice said.

"Nor do I," Roberts said. "The audience has not come prepared spend the night. They've arrived full of curiosity. So, let us walk and talk awhile and see if we can do what can't be done."

"Dear me, spare us," Voice said, "Genealogies of the dead, towns and places long forgotten. Let's forget it and just sing and dance."

Roberts ignored the comment and looked out at the crowd. "The drama of redemption unfolds over a great stretch of time," he said. "Within the broad swath of history, characters play their parts; they come and go. Their lines are embedded in the chronicles. We see their faces. We know their proclivities. We internalize. We sympathize. We criticize.

"Frozen in time, they remain alive most dramatically. They speak to us tellingly yet unknowingly. The righteous and rotten speak their lines. The wounded and wicked play their parts. They move from scene to scene. Some move under cover of darkness; others in broad daylight.

To everything there is a season, and a time to every purpose under the heaven:
A time to weep, and a time to laugh; a time to mourn, and a time to dance . . .

"There was a time of year when kings went off to war, and the year when King David did not go. We see his face. We internalize. We criticize. We sympathize. King David is a character who wept, laughed, mourned, and danced.

"His lines live, begetting truth. 'The Lord is my shepherd,' he testified. The king also said, 'The Lord said unto my Lord, sit thou at my right hand, until I make thine enemies thy footstool.'

"In the great drama known as Pentecost, St. Peter drew upon that line, quoting it. Oh yes, words and lines sourced divine have a great propensity to intertwine. They mingle and bind, projecting even greater meaning than they did apart.

"Yes, yes, to everything there is a season. There's 'a time to keep silent and a time to speak.' To which I add, a time to exegete a passage and a time to ponder the whole. Fragments enough we have. Yes, yes, the drama can easily be lost amid the lines—and with it the wonder of divine choreography. Indeed, 'the Bible is a long book, bursting with miracles, wonders and marvels."[58]

As I looked on from row five, it dawned on me. Roberts had no intention of switching the performance mode.

"Let us address the topic at hand, redemption's divine choreography, not by pushing it. No, no, let's adore and admire it by what we weave, stitch, and clip away. First let's do a bit of clipping."

"I told you," Inquisitor said. "Clipping the Holy Writ—we're doomed."

"Patience," Sojourner said. "It's an illustration, not humiliation of the Word."

Roberts acknowledged not a word. Instead, with his blue eyes open wide, he stared into the balcony. Then he broke off his stare and stepped over to the Holy Writ placed upon the music stand. He took hold of one of the gold ribbons draped over the open Bible and swiftly lifted it away.

"Yes, let us strip dreams and visions from the Holy Writ. Oracle, bring forth the scissors and let us clip."

Still holding the gold ribbon in his hand, Roberts stepped over to the table under the light. Oracle rose to join him, clutching a large pair of metal scissors. The scissors had long, shiny blades and black handles. The blades glistened in the light.

"Oracle," Roberts said, "take the end of the ribbon and let us clip properly, but not gleefully. Sojourner, Voice, and Inquisitor, join us; bring your boxes. Think of the biblical dreams we might dare to clip away. We'll do so randomly."

Sojourner placed his box next to Oracle, who stood stage left of the table. Voice and Inquisitor positioned their boxes behind Roberts.

"OK, with everyone settled, let's clip," Roberts said. "I'll start. You know, Joel's prophecy concerning dreams and visions. Sorry, Prophet Joel, but your words are now null and void. You prophecy has ceased. No spirit pouring out on prophesying daughters. Old men shall not dream dreams; young men shall not see visions. Clip!"

Oracle clipped off a piece of ribbon some three inches long. Roberts and the troupe watched as the golden piece fluttered down into the basket.

"I like dreams," Voice said.

"Yes, Voice, we all do, but not everyone does. Some people relegate dreams to dreams and nothing more. They'd rather not ponder too deeply the matter of dreams laced in and through the Holy Writ. The dreams speak of God mysteriously engaged, of divine choreography beyond simplified reduction.

"Now let's go along to Egypt," Roberts said.

"So very far away," Sojourner said.

"We'll go to a dungeon," Roberts said.

"Worse," Sojourner said.

"We just entered," Roberts said. "What do you see, Sojourner? Peer. You've visited this drama before."

"Well, I suppose that must be Joseph standing with two of Pharaoh's prisoners."

"Yes, I see them too," Inquisitor said.

"Listen," Roberts said. "Joseph is asking them a question. Oracle, interpret for us."

"Joseph asked, 'Wherefore look ye so sadly today?'" Oracle said. "And they replied, 'We have dreamed a dream, and there is no interpreter of it.' And Joseph said, 'Tell me the dreams, I pray you.'"

"Those wee lines rest at the heart of divine choreography," Roberts said.

"Yes, but do you really want to put your stock in dreams?" Voice asked.

"The question is: do you want to put your stock in the Holy Writ?" Roberts asked. "Dreams and visions punctuate the whole of the Holy Writ. 'We have dreamed a dream.' I love that line, those words. Oracle, remind us of the dreams."

"Well," Oracle said, "the butler dreamed of three branches sprouting grapes, which he pressed into Pharaoh's cup. The baker dreamed of three baskets full of bread. Then Joseph interpreted their dreams, revealing their fate. In three days the baker was dead, while the Pharaoh drank wine from the butler's cup."

"A butler and a baker dreamed a dream that tells a tale," Roberts said.

"Whose tale? What else, Oracle?"

"In time," Oracle said, "Pharaoh, too, dreamed a dream, one no one could interpret. Then the butler remembered his omission in forgetting Joseph in the dungeon; Joseph then was summarily summoned to Pharaoh's court. The rest is history."

"Yes, but whose history?" Roberts said. Clip! "Let's carry on clipping visions and dreams. Who recalls one or the other? Each will be followed with Oracle's clip."

"Then let's not forget Joseph," Inquisitor said. "Wasn't he the greatest dreamer of them all? Oh, how his brothers hated his dream of bowing sheaves." Clip!

"Jacob's stairway to heaven," Sojourner said. Clip!

"Isaiah's vision of God on his throne with the seraphs calling out and door posts trembling," Voice said. Clip!

In like succession the clipping carried on. King Nebuchadnezzar's dazzling enormous statue—clip! Gideon's tumbling loaf of barley bread striking the Midian camp—clip! Belshazzar's knocking knees when he saw the handwriting on the wall—clip!

"I know," Voice said. "Joseph's angelic dream telling him not to dismiss Mary, to whom he was betrothed." Clip!

"We mustn't forget Samuel," Roberts said. "The ardent child who would not stay asleep, but responded to the call." Clip!

"Or Daniel," Inquisitor said. "The Holy Writ claims he stood on the river bank and saw 'a man clothed in linen, whose loins were girded with gold of Uphaz.'" Clip!

"Ezekiel," Voice said. "He saw dry bones rattling on the ground, prophesied over them, and they rose as a great host."

"Yes," Roberts said, "for the sake of illustration, reluctantly we must." Clip!

Roberts continued, "St. Peter, it's said you heard, 'Rise, Peter; kill, and eat,' but still, we must clip away the floating sheet." Clip!

"St. Paul, on the Damascus road—no one else heard 'Saul, Saul, why persecutest thou me?' Too mysterious, we must." Clip!

"Ananias, sorry, we're pulling your act from Acts, blotting out your vision. Besides, no one else has ever seen scales fall from someone's eyes." Clip!

"Sorry, most of all, John, your entire revelation is gone."[59] Clip!

"Isn't that better?" Roberts said. "We could carry on, but we've clipped away a good bit of weighty weight. We've embraced modernity, while visions and dreams cling to antiquity.

"Oracle, there's another line, a most compelling line, now that we're in a clipping mood; let's clip that too. Won't you kindly recite it?"

"Do you refer to the line laced into the text of Romans?" Oracle asked.

"Yes, that's the one," Roberts said.

"It goes like this," Oracle said. "'For whatsoever things were written aforetime were written for our learning, that we through patience and comfort of the scriptures might have hope.'" Clip!

"And there's another of a similar vein," Oracle said.

"Let's hear it," Roberts said.

Oracle said, "'If there be a prophet among you, I the Lord will make myself known unto him in a vision, and will speak unto him in a dream.'"

"Yes, I see," Roberts said. "But I don't think we should clip it."

No dream I might have dreamed could matched the scene I watched from my seat in row five. I thought, "Who is this man that turns the mind upside down and challenges it to right itself?"

With the first gold ribbon scissored away, Bevin Roberts stepped over and lifted another from Oracle's Holy Writ. Three gold ribbons and the red one remained draped over the sacred book. The ribbons extended a foot or so over the top and bottom of the stand, swaying gently with the breeze drifting in the hall.

"Oracle, we must move on to the angels," Roberts said.

"Wait!" Voice shouted. "We mustn't!"

"We mustn't what?" Roberts asked.

"We mustn't clip away the angels," Voice said. "I love angels as much as dreams."

"The dreams are gone," Roberts said. "Let's move along to another spot; perhaps we'll see things a bit differently."

Roberts motioned to a set of boxes downstage on the right. Without objection, Inquisitor, Voice, and Sojourner made the move to their new seats. Once settled, Roberts looked toward the balcony, and with the voice of a master orator, he said, "Gabriel, wondrous celestial being, humbly we inquire, when did you receive the call to call upon the Virgin Mary when you did?"

As Roberts stood there with open arms, a number of people in the audience turned and looked for Gabriel. He continued, "Was it the very day, the day before, an hour, a year, or more? It's true, I know; I believe it's so, what the Holy Writ says of you.

"To Nazareth in Galilee you were sent, to Mary, the chosen one of God. How does the process of sending go? Is it a process brief or more elaborate? By the way, how many languages do angels speak? No one knows, but I suppose you speak them all.

"The Holy Writ captures your lines, 'And the angel came in unto her, and said, Hail, thou that art highly favoured, the Lord is with thee: blessed art thou among women.' You bore words the world had longed to hear.

"As Isaiah said, 'For since the beginning of the world men have not heard, nor perceived by the ear, neither hath the eye seen, O God, beside thee, what he hath prepared for him that waiteth for him.'

"Yet you announced the one prepared, the one ears would hear and eyes would see. Never had the world witnessed such a perfect union of medium and message.[60]

"Gabriel, we dare not clip you away; rather, we'll fold this golden ribbon and lay it gently near the altar, symbolizing the host of angels that populate the Holy Writ. All of them messengers, though we know not your number.

"Gabriel, lower than you we are made; this we know. How much lower we do not know. We are raising here the matter of redemption's divine choreography. There are many who like biblical bits but tend to shy away from its true conception. Surely the Holy Writ is full of mystery.

"Concerning your number, Jacob said he saw angels ascending and descending along the holy ladder, which we just clipped away. Just the same, is the ladder still in place? No one knows how these matters go.

"And in the ancient narrative of Job, we read telling lines about angels. God said to Job, 'Where wast thou when I laid the foundations of the earth? When the morning stars sang together, and all the angels shouted for joy?'

"I suppose you and Archangel Michael were there, in that number.

"And again to numbers, on the night when Jesus Christ was handed over to the mob, he said, 'Thinkest thou that I cannot now pray to my Father, and he shall presently give me more than twelve legions of angels?'

"And John the Revelator, whose vision we also clipped away, claimed, 'I beheld, and I heard the voice of many angels round about the throne . . . and the number of them was ten thousand times ten thousand, and thousands of thousands.'

"Yes, yes, no, no, no more clipping, Gabriel. I dare say if we cut much more away, the drama would not exist. We would possess a mere play and not a drama of prophetic prose."

"Sir Roberts," Inquisitor said, "do you believe angels are as active as once they were?"

Roberts raised his right arm and pointed toward a pair of large doors rigged between the rafters. From row five, I could see them well. They looked like old barn or stable doors with big black hinges.

"Open," Roberts said.

Immediately the doors sprung open, releasing thousands of gold ribbon cuttings that fluttered down and across the hall.

"Clasp one," Roberts said. "Remember the day that a gold ribbon floated down upon you in Anselm Hall."

The ribbon cuttings descended all along every row in the hall, including number five. Enthusiasm swept through the audience. Arms reached, hands clasped, fingers snatched, and faces smiled. A cutting the size of a small bookmark landed upon my knee. I smiled and clutched it.

Roberts wasted little time as the freefall of ribbons began to settle down. He stepped over to the Holy Writ and lifted another gold ribbon. Once again, as an orator, he began to speak.

"Prophecies of the Nazarene, the Son of God, the Son of man, the Word made flesh, we now embrace. In the Holy Writ they rest, very much alive. How did they get there, these prophecies alive? Apart through culture, time, and space, together they are mysteriously woven in.

"Clip them we dare not. Cherish them we must. What do they say? Listen to the prophet Zechariah, who helps tell the tale:

'Rejoice greatly, O people of Zion! Shout in triumph, O people of

Jerusalem! Look, your king is coming to you. He is righteous and victorious, yet he is humble, riding on a donkey—even on a donkey's colt.'

"Inquisitor, please bring the crimson yarn and be our stitcher. Oracle and I will hold the golden ribbon taut while you stitch a crimson stitch for every prophecy read. Stitch!"

Oracle reached into one of the boxes and produced the crimson yarn, along with a needle longer than his hand. He held the needle between his thumb and forefinger. A long loop of crimson yarn passed through the needle's eye.

With an obvious rounding motion of his arm and shoulder, Inquisitor stitched a crimson stitch for the prophecy Roberts had just read.

And so it went . . . Oracle would recite, and Roberts would say, "Stitch."

"'But you, O Bethlehem Ephrathah, who are little to be among the clans of Judah, from you shall come forth for me one who is to be ruler in Israel, whose origin is from of old, from ancient days.'"

"Stitch!"

"'When Israel was a child, I loved him, and out of Egypt I called my son.'"

"Stitch!"

On the second stitch, the crowd joined in. Just a single word, but it sounded so dramatic when hundreds of people in unison said, "Stitch!"

"'He hath poured out his soul unto death: and he was numbered with the transgressors; and he bare the sin of many, and made intercession for the transgressors.'"

"Stitch!"

"'But he was wounded for our transgressions; he was bruised for our iniquities: the chastisement of our peace was upon him, and with his stripes we are healed.'"

"Stitch!"

"'You brought me up from the grave, O Lord. You kept me from falling into the pit of death.'"

"Stitch!"

With more than two dozen verses read and stitched away, Roberts said, "Sojourner, the silver chest, please, so we can stow the stitched ribbon away."

Sojourner quickly disappeared into the wings and then reemerged holding a small silver chest. In terms of size, the chest resembled the width of a shoe box, but twice as tall and with a rounded top. Sojourner opened the lid, lowered the box, and Oracle softly placed the stitched ribbon inside.

"The needle and crimson yarn as well," Roberts said. Inquisitor looped the yarn into a small ball and carefully placed the needle and yarn upon the ribbon. Sojourner closed the lid, turned around, and silently walked away.

The troupe looked on, as Sojourner disappeared into the wing, stage right. In no time, he reappeared without the chest.

Roberts said, "Sojourner, you've returned without the staff."

"Yes, indeed," Sojourner said. "I'll fetch it."

Sojourner briskly departed and returned with a long wooden shepherd's staff.

"That's a fine looking staff," Roberts said, as Sojourner placed it in his hand. "Quite old, very nice—where did you get it?" Roberts asked.

"Well, it's yours," Sojourner said.

"So it is," Roberts replied. "The staff presses upon my mind the matter of miracles. How would the drama divine fare without them? Not fare at all—they set the grand narrative apart from all other works. Though modern technical wizardry tries to emulate dimensions three and one.

"Still, a leper healed is a leper healed. Let us wind our ribbon round the staff. This particular gold ribbon has miracles inscribed in fine calligraphy. Voice, please begin winding the ribbon around the staff, starting at the tip, and pause when you have covered a foot or so."

Roberts held the staff upright while Voice knelt on his knees and began to wind. He circled the tip with three tight, overlapping wraps before slanting his successive winds. When he had covered well over a foot, he paused. Inquisitor knelt on his right knee and gently placed the ribbon between his fingers. He squinted and read, "Naaman of Aram."

"Yes, yes," Roberts said. "Naaman of Syria, beset by leprosy. He balked when Elisha told him what to do, but he then recanted. After seven dips in the Jordan, his flesh was free of leprosy. Wind Naaman in!"

With Naaman wound around the staff, Inquisitor peered again and read, "Widow of Zarephath."

"Yes," Roberts said. "A poor widow picking sticks, she and her son were destitute and prepared to die. Even so, the widow listened to Elijah's words and survived. Her store of meal and oil mysteriously resupplied. Wind the widow in!"

Again the audience took part, but not knowing exactly what Roberts would say, they lagged just a fraction behind. Somehow this made them end the quip on a louder note.

"Widow's son," Inquisitor read.

"Oh yes, that too," Roberts said. "Later on the widow's son fell dead. Elijah stretched himself upon the child three times and prayed. The body was no longer dead. Wind in the widow's son!"

Still kneeling on one knee, Inquisitor said, "Yes, let me see . . . blind Bartimaeus—that's the name I see."

"Blind Bartimaeus cried out as Jesus passed. Though the crowd said, 'Hush,' Jesus bid him come. The blind beggar begged for sight. By faith, sight he found. Wind Bartimaeus in!"

"Hezekiah next I read," Inquisitor said.

"Nigh unto death Hezekiah was, till Isaiah placed a poultice of figs upon him. God added fifteen years to his span of life. Wind Hezekiah in!"

"Centurion," Inquisitor said.

"Such a story," Roberts said. "A certain centurion went to Jesus and said, 'I am not worthy for you to come under my roof, but just speak the word, and my servant shall be healed. Jesus Christ was astonished by his remarkable faith. The servant was healed that very hour. The centurion, along with his servant—wind them in!"

"Not sure," Inquisitor said. "The next bit of calligraphy reads 'Many Brought.'"

"'Tis right," Roberts said. "Yes, this must be a verse from Matthew's Gospel. I believe it goes like this: 'When the evening arrived, they brought unto him many possessed with devils: and he cast out the spirits with his word, and healed all that were sick.' Many brought—wind them in. Who's next?"

"Withered," Inquisitor replied.

"Withered—I know one," Roberts said. "Must be him. 'In a synagogue on a Sabbath day, Jesus saw a man with a withered hand,' his right in fact.

Jesus said, 'Stretch out your hand.' Withered did so, and his hand was restored. Wind Withered in.

"Let's have two, if we might," Roberts said.

"Touch and Great Multitudes," Inquisitor replied.

"Touch," Roberts said. "The hem of his garment—Touch touched. Great Multitudes just like the Many Brought, but not the same . . ."

And thus they carried on, with Inquisitor reading names written in the ribbon of gold and Voice winding them round the staff. Up, up, the gold ribbon spiraled. Damsel, daughter of Jairus, Lazarus whom Jesus loved, the man among the tombs that everyone feared . . . around the shepherd's staff, Voice wound them in.

The exercise had a spellbinding effect on the crowd. Certainly no one had ever seen costumed men winding a gold ribbon of miracles round a shepherd's staff.

I thought, "The novelty of the act forces the mind to embrace what's known in patterns new. Nothing is one-dimensional, flat and factual. I'm watching something very rich taking place upon the stage."

After a while, though, my mind would whirl and revert to what I knew, not just what I saw. I'd remind myself that Roberts founded the ancient Order of Message Makers in 1637. What I knew and what I saw made me feel that I knew nothing at all.

Anyway, soon the staff went the way of the basket, silver chest, and gold ribbon with crimson twine. Waiting for what would appear next, no one waited long. As soon as the staff vanished, a huge wreath tied to silk straps slowly descended from the rafters. The wreath originated from the same opening that had sent the gold ribbon cuttings fluttering down across the hall.

The wreath, seemingly constructed of mature grapevines, extended to a width twice that of the table. The white silk straps, four in all, extended up into the darkened area beyond the ceiling joists. A spotlight, positioned in the middle of the dark space, shone down through the center of the wreath. The shaft of light illuminated the silk straps, transforming them into streams of light.

With the wreath hovering about a meter and a half above the table,

Roberts stepped forward and lifted the final gold ribbon from the sacred text. Surprisingly, the single ribbon had three layers, which allowed Inquisitor, Voice, and Sojourner to each receive a gold ribbon from Roberts.

With their ribbons in hand, Roberts asked them to place the boxes around the table so they could reach the wreath. They each grabbed a box, placed it upside down, and quickly stood on top of it. Voice, the shortest of the three, selected a taller box. Inquisitor, the tallest, found a flat box about the height of a short step. Each held their gold ribbon and awaited Roberts' instruction.

"Now we come to the final gold ribbon illustration, underscoring the extraordinary feat of redemption's divine choreography. We shall weave acts of wonder into our wreath."

"What do you mean, acts of wonder?" Voice asked.

"Acts that could not have happened without divine intervention," Roberts said. "Many they are; only a few we shall mention. I will walk round you, and as I do, I will call out an act, in no particular order. Our aim is not chronology, but choreography. As the old saying goes, one may speak of the sunrise before it rises and its setting before it sets.

"With each act mentioned, small or large, you are to weave it in. Weave to the right, lacing your gold ribbons amidst the vines. Each of you shall cover a third of the wreath, eventually catching up to the ribbon weaver ahead of you. When you need to move your boxes, do so, not waiting for my instruction. Move along spryly, as ribbon weavers should.

"So, an act to start—which one shall it be? Let it be the shadow that stepped backwards down the stairs. King Hezekiah believed that on his deathbed he laid until the prophet Isaiah told him otherwise; he said God had granted him another fifteen years. King Hezekiah asked Isaiah for affirmation. The sign? A shadow taking ten backward steps down the stairs. Weave!"

With the first "Weave" uttered, the audience took their cue, so I knew the second weave would certainly produce a resounding "Weave!"

"A furnace stoked seven times hotter than its normal roar to receive Shadrach, Meshach, and Abednego. Yet when Nebuchadnezzar leapt to his feet and peered inside, he saw the three dancing with a most peculiar man. Weave!

"Charioted horses galloped into the sea gone dry until the sea went back to being a sea again. Weave!

"A discarnate hand wrote mene, mene, tekel, parsin on Belshazzar's wall. How does a hand know how to spell? Weave!

"Elisha—one wonders what he thought when he witnessed the ax head float up to the waters' top. Weave!

"Amid the darkness a firepot and blazing torch passed between carcasses prepared. Not a dream but a scene choreographed by God, as Abraham slept unaware. Weave!

"Moses saw a bush burning away, which mysteriously did not burn away. The bush had roots in sacred soil. Weave!

"In the evening quails came up and covered the camp, and in the morning dew lay round about the camp. When the dew had gone, a flake-like thing, as fine as hoarfrost, covered the ground. The Israelites called the fine, flake-like thing 'manna.' Weave!

"Locusts, frogs, and hail could provide us with triple weaves, but let's weave in water flowing from a rock instead. Weave!

"Are we to believe the sun and moon actually halted in the sky? Yes, indeed, and make that a double weave! Weave!

"How does a virgin bear . . ."

Roberts kept circling and casting out his lines, as his spry weavers weaved their golden ribbons amidst the wreath of vines.

His final casts took in the curtain rent, darkness blotting out the sun, and the walking dead, the ones that entered Jerusalem surprisingly alive.

Roberts wove in Christ's resurrection well before the walking dead. As he said, his lines would not be sequential. Instead, with cadence he juggled the acts that pressed upon his mind.

Roberts didn't look up at the wreath until he had cast those final lines. When he did, he seemed quite pleased. The three gold ribbons touched perfectly end to end. No overlapping and no gaps between—just the appearance of a single gold ribbon woven through the vines as one.

"Very nice, indeed," Roberts said.

The three weavers stepped off their boxes, picked them up, and carried them away. Oracle, along with three, stepped back upstage, distancing themselves from Roberts, who moved to the podium, lifting the crimson ribbon from the Holy Writ. Before he reached for the ribbon, he stood quite still, staring down at the sacred text and the crimson ribbon running through it.

Minus an audience to concern him, I felt he could have stood there indefinitely. Then, at the instant of his choosing, he clasped the crimson ribbon and swiftly stepped back several paces. At that point, a broad drape of crimson cloth unfurled from the rafters and extended to a height just above the grapevine wreath. The cloth's width nearly equaled that of the wreath.

I watched a gentle, rolling wave pulse from top to bottom of the broad crimson cloth laced with thin ribbons of gold. Nothing mechanical or rigged aided the motion; the banner simply submitted to a soft current of air. The waving pulse would begin at the top and flow down through the banner. When one wave disappeared, another would emerge and ripple along the same trail of descent.

Two lights beamed down from the ceiling loft, sending shafts of light along either side of the cloth. The lighted crimson cloth looked especially stunning hanging inside the luminous white silk straps tethered to the wreath.

In a manner not lacking drama, Roberts said, "So amidst the flow of miracles, angels, prophecies, and acts of wonder, the central character of the universe stepped onstage. Yes, yes, indeed he did. In the fullness of time, redemption's divine choreography revealed the redeemer. Surprise, to a world of watching eyes, the dramatist himself took center stage in the drama. He assumed the part no one else could possibly play.

"No, no, no audition took place for the redeemer's role. Who else could pick up a cross and become a living, dying crucifix? Such a way to die, the way you died, a spectacle on display before the world's watching eyes.

"The cast, the crowd, so cruel; like Judas they possessed co-opted hearts. Their mouths spoke not lines rehearsed, but words inspired by intent of evil. Even so, their sinful ways and words you forgave.

"Surely you could have done what the crowd jeered: "He saved others; let him save himself, *if* he is the Christ of God, his Chosen One!" That little conjunction *if*, though, did not bait you. It failed, just as it did at the time of the tempter's temping. There is no *if* when the article is real.

"Unquestionably you could 'have come down from the cross,' as they shouted, but then you would not been who you claimed to be, the redeemer in the great drama of divine choreography. Heaven's host surely knelt and wept as the worldly crowd gloated and watched you die.

"You had to die; we were dead but wanted to live. We needed redemption by a redeemer who redeems. Dear Lord, we needed you!"

At that point Roberts paused and looked up. Then, to everyone's amazement, without accompaniment, he began to sing:

Be Thou my vision, oh Lord of my heart
Nought be all else to me, save that Thou art
Thou my best thought by day or by night
Waking or sleeping, Thy presence my light

At this juncture, the troupe joined him, gathering around him in the center of the stage. Together they sang on:

Be Thou my wisdom, and Thou my true word
I ever with Thee and Thou with me Lord
Thou my great father and I Thy true son
Thou in me dwelling and I with Thee one

Then those in the audience who had not already joined in joined in and sang on:

Riches I need not, nor man's empty praise
Thou mine inheritance now and always
Thou and Thou only first in my heart
High King of heaven my treasure
Thou art

At which point everyone in Anselm Hall rose to their feet, along with me in row five. Together we sang:

High King of heaven, my victory won
May I reach heaven's door, bright heaven sun
Heart of my own heart, whatever befall
Still be my vision, oh ruler of all

With a single line lingering, the troupe bowed, waved, and Bevin Roberts said, "Thank you! We love you one and all. Good-bye, everyone. Good-bye, Anselm Hall."

After that, they walked offstage, as the audience sang on:

Still be my vision, oh ruler of all . . .

CHAPTER TWELVE
The Manuscript

As Roberts and the troupe exited the stage, I quickly slipped out of row five and headed toward the small stairway at the bottom of the aisle stage right. The steps led to a wing of dressing rooms, including a room allocated for scripts. When I reached the steps, I paused and looked across the hall.

As the audience continued to sing, I spotted Fr. McQuince making his way to the front. He looked quite pleased; I wondered what he would say. Most everyone had risen to their feet and were looking to the stage, where the mystical banner continued its slow, pulsing wave.

I turned away and ascended the short flight of steps. My heart pounded. Scattered thoughts filled my head. I advanced by instinct, not knowing what to say. Into the wing I stepped; to my immediate right I saw the door. In letters painted black, the words *Script Room* stood out prominently on the faded white door.

In front of the door I paused, thinking I should run, but my instinct moved my hand to knock. Twice I knocked, quickly, more softly than not.

"Please come in," spoke a voice on the opposite side. I turned the handle, not knowing if the mystery world in which I abided would vaporize beneath my feet. The thought vanished as I stepped through the doorway onto a floor of squeaky planks.

There he stood. "I like the sound of floors that squeak with you as you pass," Roberts said. "What about you?"

"Yes, yes," I said, as I shook his extended hand.

"Squeaking floors remind us of time passing, and that we pass through where others have passed," Robert said.

141

"Yes," I said.

"Speaking of passing," he said. "The troupe has moved along . . . how shall I put it . . . rather rapidly. I'll join them once we've said what it is we shall say."

"Sure," I said.

I looked at the corner of the room. On a small table sat the silver chest and next to it, the crimson-stitched ribbon. The gold-ribboned staff leaned against the wall in the corner, and on the floor was the basket of ribbon pieces.

As I looked in awe, Roberts stepped to the far side of the room, where rolled scripts filled a bank of shelves that extended from the ceiling to the floor. "This one caught my eye," he said, as he pulled the script from a shoulder-high cubicle.

"Macbeth—no doubt you know it," Roberts said. "I love the play, its telling lines. I nearly met Shakespeare once, when I was quite young and he was old. Though he never grew *that* old. We were running through the market stalls, when he came walking through. I approached the entourage roundabout him, but I found myself shewed away. I did receive, however, a notice from his eyes.

"Words forming lines—Shakespeare knew how to mold them exceedingly well. No doubt he prayed many a time over his quill. Listen to these lines he placed on the lips of Banquo, spoken to Macbeth:

> *'The instruments of darkness tell us truths,*
> *Win us with honest trifles, to betray's*
> *In deepest consequence.'*[61]

"So true, so very true," Roberts said.

"Yes," said I.

"And these words spoken by Macbeth:

> *'Come what come may,*
> *Time and the hour runs through the roughest day.'*[62]

"Narrative, come what may, I will soon be on my way . . . and you are here to stay."

"You mean here, in this state?" I asked.

"Yes, here, but no, not in this state," he said. "Normality is about to reach you, but remember, normality belongs to time, and the hours are filled with matters of eternal consequence. Right, right, so right you are to cast your eyes through the lines and discover the world of redemption's divine choreography. Peering beyond the lines adds richness, fuller meaning, and depth to the storyline.

"The world needs a non-world perspective in order to grasp the wonder of the world. The greatest masters of the Holy Writ know they are not masters. A key does not place the treasure in the chest; it merely locks and unlocks the store. In your day and age, there are many instruments of darkness telling truths while avoiding truth.

"It's time to look behind the curtain—not just any curtain anywhere, but the curtain torn—and consider the epic feat of divine choreography. There we see a sure and steadfast anchor of the soul, a hope that enters the inner shrine behind the curtain, where Jesus has gone as a forerunner on our behalf. He, of course, is our great high priest after the order of Melchizedek.

"Advancement can carry genius appeal, tricking the naive by what they see. 'Technology enchants.'[63] Images appear minus a message. The Word became flesh and dwelt among us. When we fix our eyes on him, and surely we can, we see not just an image but the image bearer.

The Son of God, in dialogue with the world—in his supremacy we see the truth of divine choreography. 'He is the radiance of the glory of God and the exact imprint of his nature, and he upholds the universe by the word of his power.'

"Drama never knew greater drama than that carried out by the Son. Such deep truth abides in his words everlasting, yet did he not say, 'My words are not my own.'

"Narrative, we must go now; walk with me. But before we go, here, take from me this crimson ribbon."

"Yes, sure," I said, as he placed it in my hand.

We walked down the hall, opened the exit door, and as soon as we stepped outside, Bevin Roberts vanished. I looked to my left, to my right, all around, but I knew in my heart what had taken place.

"What am I to do?" I thought. Truly, my spirit had leaped within me as I listened to him speak. A great weight had lifted. I wanted to shout, walk, and pray.

I progressed down the high street, along the stretch where Platform, Discarnate, and Rejection had set up their displays. Not a semblance of their presence existed, no stakes or leaflets left behind. No signs, no stages—the space they once occupied boasted an array of flower stalls. I smiled and mused, paused, and then continued.

As I passed in front of the final flower stall, a voice beside me said, "They fled before dawn. Never saw characters in such a rush. Anyhow, do you like sunflowers? Look at that lovely bunch reaching for the sky. Beautiful, don't you think?"

The voice belonged to Mr. Kind.

He said, "Let's just keep walking, and as we do, we shall do a bit of talking."

We took some half-dozen steps, saying nothing. He knew I needed to absorb his presence. He sensed my spiritual state and the ruminations running through my mind. Mr. Kind said, "Let's us walk toward the port; the sun is setting."

"Sure," I said. "But I wonder . . ."

"Let's talk first of lesser matters," he said, "such as chimney tops and brick patterns."

So we walked along, talking not about all that had transpired, but instead the architectural features of the shops and structures we passed.

"Lovely copper roof," he said. "And that magnificent window, that one with the diamond-shaped panes . . ."

"Yes," I said.

I merely listened as Mr. Kind carried on as a very unique tour guide, pointing out distinctive characteristics of the man-made structures. A sense of genuine fascination undergirded his numerous observations.

As we neared the port, I heard shouting. We saw a crowd, and as we neared, I recognized Charley James standing in a circle of people two and three rows deep. He seemed nearly beside himself. He'd speak and then shriek a bit, shake his head, and continue speaking.

Butcher Crombie, a rather large fellow, said, "Now calm down, Charley, from the top; tell us what you actually saw."

"OK, OK," Charley said. "I was standing right there at the harbor where the crafts is always tied. You know, the north plank side, when it happened. I wasn't more than a couple of meters from the boat, the rowboat them theatrical fellows came in on.

"Go ahead and say I'm nuts, but you wasn't there; I was. The rope untied itself. I don't mean the boat came untied; I mean the rope untied itself. As quiet as a sleeping rabbit, the rope all of sudden began to unwind itself from the nautical. Round and round the rope unwound, rising higher with each wind unwound.

"Next the rope flung itself through the air, into the boat, and dropped down. Then, deary me, my soul is not lying, the side of the rowboat tipped once, then once again, and began to wobble from side to side. I seen it—several times it tipped, wobbled, and bobbed.

"Jesus be my witness, what I saw, I saw. Four pairs of oars, the old wooden type, sprung into position and began to row the vessel away. First astern, then the boat swung ahead toward the sea. Not person in sight—just oars rowing back and forth in the water with one accord."

"Come on, Charley," said an older, white-haired gentleman standing in the inner circle.

"You don't need to believe me," Charley said. "The truth of what I seen is in what I seen. I watched, dumfounded, totally awestruck, as the empty vessel rowed away from the harbor. I yelled out at it, not knowing what to say. Something like, 'Hey boat, hey boat, hey!' But the vessel just kept rowing away.

"Then, about halfway out to the mist, I saw a mirage. I shook my head and looked intently at what it was. It was him, the lead fellow of that message-making troupe. Upright, there he sat in the bow, alone, and with his back as erect as a mast, he looked toward the port.

"As the oars kept rowing, I seen him begin to wave. He waved slowly, with his right hand. I looked across the waters, then back again. He continued to wave as the vessel neared the mist. I waved back, in a manner like his, but his eyes on me were not fixed. Then into the mist the vessel slipped."

"'Tis so what one can see," said Mr. Kind, "when in the mind there is more than matter."

As Charley carried on answering questions, Mr. Kind said, "Let's pull away and walk toward the monastery."

At that juncture Mr. Kind's jovial countenance gave way to a wise and concerning posture.

"Do you recall in my note the line, 'Once upon a time, I coached a learned soul, under the cover of night?'"

"Yes," I said.

"Well, the sun has set, and night proceeds to what tomorrow holds," he said. "Tomorrow will not be another day like today. I also said in my note, 'Through a mirror dimly you presently peer, but be not dismayed, clarity will surely dawn. Exist in your state of multiplicity until the multiplicity no longer exists.'

"Your state of multiplicity is slipping away, but what you've seen and heard will linger long . . . lifelong. There is so much more to see than what the naked eye can see, so much more to tell. St. Paul pledged that he could not tell the more he saw. Yet does his gallant apostleship not speak of what he saw?"

"I understand," I said, "but Bevin Roberts and the troupe . . . what I've witnessed . . . it's so utterly surreal."

"Yes, I know," he said. "Consider, though, what Peter, James, and John beheld when Moses and Elijah spoke with the transfigured Christ. It is not up to angels and men to prescribe the thin space God commands.

"The lane is ahead. I so delight in the luminous pools of light that light the way. As we come around the bend, I must bend away. I must be about the work assigned. The reapers need a bit of help in sharpening their sickles.

"Oh yes, the case you brought with you to All Saints—you will find it under your desk in the cove. We're here, it seems. Walk on, Narrative; you have much to tell, so tell it well."

I knew the moment of inevitability had arrived. No more comments, no more questions, so I simply said, "Good-bye, Mr. Kind."

"Good-bye, Narrative," he said. "Walk on. Tell it well."

And then through the luminous rings I began to pass. One by one, my shadow also passed. In the middle of the lane, I had a compulsion to turn around, but I didn't. I walked on. Before I reached the final ring and passed it through, I felt the knots of my habit rope bouncing about my knees.

"My habit," I thought; "I never want to shed it again." I felt the smooth rope of silk and, for some reason, recalled Bewilderment's twine. I smiled a smile that did not fall away.

As I entered the monastery grounds, I saw the brothers gathered round the fire pit on the eastern lawn. Through the shadows I approached, spotting them all—Epic, Saga, Plot, Writer, Drama, and Story—then they spotted me.

"We're just setting off for a moonlight stroll among the trails," Story said. "I'm delighted you've decided to join us; you've literally locked yourself away these last number of days. Anyway, we want to chat about a play, on the theme of redemption, and we wonder if you might have any creative ideas."

"Yes, sure," I said. "I'll go. I just need to check something in my room."

"Nar," Writer said, "what's that red ribbon protruding from your pouch?"

"Oh, that, yes," I said. I pulled the ribbon out for all to see. "Nice, isn't it?"

"Yes, quite nice, "Drama said, "very rich and vibrant, a true crimson."

"I'll return in a flash," I said. Up the stairs I bounded and took the key out of my pocket, in the manner I always had. I entered the room and headed for my desk in the narrow cove.

Beneath the desk, I saw my case, just as Mr. Kind said I would. On top of the desk, I placed my hand on a thick gold folder stuffed with my handwritten pages. I opened it. The little label that I had once stuck on the outside of the folder fell to my feet. I picked it up, and in a faint pencil scrawl, I read what I had written: "Manuscript, *Divine Choreography of Redemption*."

I placed the crimson ribbon on the manuscript and walked away, thinking, "I must tell it, and tell it well."

The End

NOTES

[1] Yuval Noah Harari, *Homo Deus: A Brief History of Tomorrow* (New York: Harper Collins, 2017) 287–88. Yuval Noah Harari links the matter of *free will* with electrochemical processes in the brain. He writes: "Next time a thought pops into your mind, stop and ask yourself: 'Why did I think this particular thought? Did I decide a minute ago to think this thought, and only then think it? Or did it just arise, without any direction or permission from me? If I am indeed the master of my thoughts and decisions, can I decide not to think about anything at all for the next sixty seconds?'"

[2] William Shakespeare, King Lear, Act 1, Scene 4.

[3] Neil Postman, *Technopoly: The Surrender of Culture to Technology* (New York: Vantage Books, 1993), 52.

[4] Postman, *Technopoly*, 71.

[5] Ellen Rose, "A Genealogy of Computer Generated Narrative" *Explorations in Media Ecology*, Volume 16 Number 1 (2017): 15.

[6] Postman, *Technopoly*, 71.

[7] Ibid., 70.

[8] Nicholas Carr, *The Glass Cage: How Our Computers Are Changing Us* (New York: W. W. Norton & Company, 2014), 17.

[9] Cheryl K. Chumley, "Saudi Arabia's New City, Neom, a Mecca for Robots," *The Washington Times*, Tuesday, October 24, 2017; Quoting Crown Prince Mohammed bin Salman, reported in *Arab News*.

[10] Sherry Turkle, *Reclaiming Conversation: The Power of Talk in a Digital Age* (New York: Penguin Press, 2015), 50.

[11] Marshall McLuhan, *Understanding Media: The Extensions of Man* (Corte Madera, California: Gingko Press, 2003), 211.

[12] Eric McLuhan, *The Sensus Communis Synesthesia and the Soul* (Toronto: BPS Books, 2015), 55–56.

[13] Nicholas Carr, *The Glass Cage: How Our Computers Are Changing Us* (New York: W. W. Norton & Company, 2014), 23.

[14] Ibid., 2.

[15] Inference to Hebrews 12:1—"Since we are surrounded by such a great cloud of witnesses, let us throw off everything that hinders . . . let us run with perseverance the race marked out for us."

[16] Marshall McLuhan, *Understanding Media: The Extensions of Man* (Corte Madera, California: Gingko Press, 2003), 333.

[17] *Reclaiming Conversation,* 130.

[18] Eric McLuhan, *The Sensus Communis Synesthesia and the Soul* (Toronto: BPS Books, 2015), 61.

[19] Eric McLuhan, *The Sensus Communis Synesthesia and the Soul* (Toronto: BPS Books, 2015), 41.

[20] Jacques Ellul, *The Presence of the Kingdom* (Colorado Springs, Col.: Helmers & Howard, 1989) 114.

[21] Hans Urs Von Balthasar, *Theo-Drama: Volume 1* (San Francisco: Ignatius Press, 1988) 20.

[22] Marshall McLuhan, *Understanding Media*, p. 68. "By continuously embracing technologies, we relate ourselves to them as servomechanisms. That is why we must, to use them at all, serve these objects, these extensions of ourselves, as gods or minor religions."

[23] William Shakespeare, *As You Like It*, Act II, Scene VII.

[24] Leo Tolstoy, *War and Peace,* (New York: Vintage Classics, Vintage Books, 2008) 1005.

[25] Fyodor Dostoevsky, *Demons* (New York: Vintage Classics, 1994), 652.

[26] Fyodor Dostoevsky, *Crime and Punishment*, (New York: Vintage Classics, 1993), 420.

[27] 2 Corinthians 12:2–5, KJV.

[28] Jacques Ellul, *The Presence of the Kingdom* (Colorado Springs, Col.: Helmers & Howard, Publishers, 1989), 104.

[29] Anselm of Canterbury, *Anselm of Canterbury: The Major Works* (Oxford: Oxford University Press, 1998, revised 2008), 208.

[30] Ibid., 210.

[31] St. Augustine, *Confessions* (New York: Barnes & Noble Classics, 2007), 106.

[32] Ibid., 100.

[33] *Anselm of Canterbury*, 270.

[34] Marshall McLuhan, *Understanding Media: The Extensions of Man* (Corte Madera, Calif.: Gingko Press,2003), 408.

[35] *Understanding Media*, 362.

[36] Jacques Ellul, *The Humiliation of the Word* (Grand Rapids, Mich.: William B. Eerdmans Publishing Co., 1985), 249.

[37] William Shakespeare, *As You Like It*, Scene VII.

[38] Ellul, *The Humiliation of the Word*, 32.

[39] Dante Alighieri, *The Divine Comedy*: (New York, Penguin Book, 2013) Canto 9, 40.

[40] *The Divine Comedy*, CANTO 34, 154–155.

[41] See interview with Kenneth Cukier, "How will big data change the way we live?" TED Radio Hour, September 9, 2016. https://www.npr.org/templates/transcript/transcript.php?storyId=492297006. "One of the most impressive areas where this concept has taken place is in the area of machine learning, OK? Machine learning is a branch of artificial intelligence which itself is a branch of computer science. The general idea is that instead of instructing a computer what to do, we are going to simply throw data at the problem and tell the computer

to figure it out for itself. And it'll help you understand it by seeing its origins." Cukier is author of *A Revolution That Will Transform How We Live, Work, and Think* and *Learning with Big Data: The Future of Education*.

[42] Marshall McLuhan, *Understanding Media: The Extensions of Man* (Corte Madera, Calif.: Gingko Press, 2003), 360. "Why does a phone ringing on the stage create instant tension?"

[43] C. S. Lewis, *The Abolition of Man* (San Francisco: Harper Collins Publishers, 2001), 81. "You cannot go on 'seeing through' things forever. The whole point of seeing through something is to see something through it."

[44] Saint Augustine, *Confessions of Saint Augustine* (New York: Barnes and Noble Books, 2007), 128.

[45] *Technopoly*, 18.

[46] Yuval Noah Harari, *Homo Deus: A Brief History of Tomorrow* (New York: Harper Collins, 2017), 391–392.

[47] Marshall McLuhan, *The Medium and the Light: Reflections on Religion*, (Eugene, Oregon: Wipf and Stock Publishers, 2010), 50. "Electric man has no bodily being. He is literally *dis*-carnate. But a discarnate world, like the one we now live in, is a tremendous menace to an incarnate Church, and its theologians haven't even deemed it worthwhile to examine the fact."

[48] Eric McLuhan, *The Sensus Communis, Synesthesia, and the Soul:* (Toronto and New York: BPS Books, 2015), 55. "The new media, then, are not manifestations of physical communication so much as manifestations of metaphysical communication. They entail the transformation of the users. Twentieth-century man—electronic man—has no lived minus a physical body for an entire century. He has become disincarnate."

[49] Neal Postman, *The End of Education* (New York: Vintage Books, 1966), 7.

[50] Job 1:6–12, KJV.

[51] Victor Hugo, *Les Miserables* (New York: Random House, 1992), 1126 [scene in which Thenardier lets Jean Valjean pass through his obscure door made of sewer grating].

[52] John Milton, *Paradise Lost,* Book I, line 263 (Mineola, New York: Dover Publications), 9.

[53] William Shakespeare, *Macbeth,* Act IV, Scene 3.

[54] Samuel T. Colridge, *The Rime of the Ancient Mariner,* Part IV (New York: The Peter Pauper Press), 21.

[55] Technological change is neither additive nor subtractive. It is ecological. I mean 'ecological' in the same sense as the word is used by environmental scientists. One significant change generates total change. If you remove the caterpillar from a given habitat, you are not left with the same environment minus caterpillars: you have a new environment, and you have reconstituted the conditions of survival. . . .

This is how the ecology of media works as well. A new technology does not add or subtract something. It changes everything. In the year 1500, fifty years after the printing press was invented, we did not have old Europe plus the printing press. We had a different Europe. After television, the United States was not America plus television; television gave a new coloration to every political campaign, to every home, to every school, to every church, to every industry. And that is why competition among media is so fierce.

[56] Yuval Noah Harari, *Homo Deus: A Brief History of Tomorrow* (New York: Harper Collins, 2017), 45-46. "For four billion years life remained confined to this tiny rock speck of a planet because natural selection made all organism utterly dependent on the unique conditions of this flying rock."

[57] Jacques Ellul, *The Technological Society* (New York: Vintage Books, 1964) 431.

[58] *Homo Deus,* 76.

[59] Ellul, *The Humiliation of the Word,* 240. "The book of Revelation is entirely constructed on the basis of visions. It is probably the highest point of apocalyptic literature, not only by virtue of its content, the strength of its thought, its continuity, and the progress of its message(whether historical-critical exegetes who are clever at slicing a text up into thin layers agree), but also because of the interpenetration and rigor of the images."

[60] Marshall McLuhan, *The Medium and the Light: Reflections on Religion* (Toronto: Stoddart, 1999), p. 103. "In Jesus Christ, there is no distance or separation between the medium and the message. It is the one case where we can say that the medium and the message are fully one and the same."

[61] *Macbeth*, Act I, Scene 3.

[62] Ibid.

[63] Sherry Turkle, *Reclaiming Conversation: The Power of Talk in a Digital Age,* (New York: Penguin Press, 2015), 13.

Lightning Source UK Ltd.
Milton Keynes UK
UKHW012134080720
366218UK00001B/24